In dedication to my mother,
Julie

1.

"Remember your penmanship says a lot about you," the mantra told to you in elementary school, junior high, or at home. Basically, by anyone who had to check your homework. It was a polite way of saying they had other things to do and rereading your worksheet was at the bottom of their priority list. I wish they would have been straightforward with it. They should have told me to clean up my act. That they didn't have time for this chicken scratch. Or at least not have said the quality of my penmanship defines my character. "Remember your penmanship allows you to share your story. It doesn't write your story." There, an approved line of encouragement. Teachers, please use generously.

I look down at my name at the top of my English paper. Shaky letters in black ink are formed to spell out Jenna Whitten. A reader would assume I'm an elementary kid. My hand starts to cramp up. I put the pen down and slowly extend my fingers. Work days are always more of a challenge. Mrs. Stark explains our first rough draft is due Monday. *Two days. I have two days to get a good start.* An introduction and the first body paragraph in other words. I adjust the paper. Positioning the pen between my index and middle finger, I'm ready to tackle this essay.

The debate topic was "Is the D.A.R.E program good for America's kids?" *D I won't do drugs. A won't have an attitude. R I will respect myself. E I will educate me.* Great, it took the other half of fifth grade to forget that song.

Well, was the program good for me? Last week I was offered pot from a boy with shaggy hair. He was wearing a drug rug. A good salesman dressed in proper attire. I pondered it for a few seconds. I turned it down.

"Is that your final answer?" he asked. I felt like I was on the game show *Want to be a Millionaire?* I timidly shook my head yes. So, what does that say? I'm still a drug virgin. That's a point for D.A.R.E. I did refer him to some freshmen though. A point for the junkies. The guy has to make his quota somehow. Maybe the government should just look into better rehab facilities.

"Well, if other high schools are anything like Valley High, D.A.R.E. should quit now." Naturally I do a facepalm as I turn my attention over to Caitlyn. I forgot to anticipate for her untimed commentary. Getting a paragraph down will be a blessing. I nod my head in agreement. My hair slips from behind my ear.

"I'm taking the same stance as you," I say through knuckles pressed against my lips. I watch her adjust her body into a pretzel-legged position in her chair. The fallen hair over my glasses is magnified in color. Rich chestnut brown strands intersect my view of her.

"Probably not a good opening sentence, but it's true." There's always a conjunction with her. 'But' seems to be her go-to. I look down at her paper. She doesn't have anything written yet either. I wish we had the same reasons for this. Hers is due to the lack of focus, whereas I am avoiding another muscle cramp from happening. I know I must get something down though before the end of class. Caitlyn is still going on about her opinion of the subject.

"The program sure as hell didn't help me in any way. If they would have brought in a couple of meth heads maybe that would have stuck with me. Or what about one of those people who speak through their necks. Would have scarred me for sure. But nope just lectures and singing the same stupid song every day." If we could use voice-to-text, her paper would be done in five minutes.

I casually go back to my paper. I nod along as she rambles. I add in an occasional murmur and furrowed brow to match her over-exaggerated frustration.

I believe that while the D.A.R.E. program has good intentions, the audience that should be most affected, being adolescents, is not saying no to drugs as much as this program is hoping to see.

Great, now I just have to get that down on paper. I look up at the clock to see it's 3:05. Other kids around me are packing up their belongings. I still have ten minutes before the final bell of the day rings. I get halfway through the word *intentions* when my hand contorts and tingles. I feel my muscles tighten. I try to push through the pain, but my penmanship suffers even more from it.

"Shit. Come on," I mutter to myself. I forfeit after finishing the word *audience*. It's 3:09. I lay my pencil flat on the desk and let its ridges knead the palm of my hand. As soon as my muscles relax, I tackle the rest of the sentence.

The bell rings as I add the *ing* to *hoping*. Caitlyn stands up in my peripheral vision. I toss the pencil down next to the paper when I finally finish the damming sentence. I go back to massaging my hand.

"Dude, only you can make writing a sport," I hear my smart-ass friend say. "Do you need an ICY Hot?" she throws in, seeing me nurture my "playing" hand.

"Shut up. Come on, it's Friday. Let's get out of this hell hole," I say, standing up.

We meet Ryan at door 12 of the high school. He greets each of us with a fist bump. I take a second to study him as he tells us about how Mr. Ellet started playing the trombone in class. His navy glasses, stereotypically enough, are the only thing about his appearance that gives credit to his smarts. Otherwise, his dark hair- a wild clump of curls- stands out against his white work t-shirt. I scan down the rest of him. Blue jeans full of stains from working on his car and a pair of beat up boots to finish off the "Ryan" look.

"I know! We could hear him from the English wing," Caitlyn exclaims. I nod along not so happy because that was another distraction.

"He should be a music teacher not a history teacher," Ryan continues.

"Yeah, if only he were good at it," I chime in trying to relax for the weekend that's now here. They both laugh in agreement.

We head for the Audi that is parked in the back of the parking lot. We slosh through the wet puddles. I feel my socks getting soaked with each step. My toes curl from the cold.

I get in the back since I rode shotgun this morning. Ryan starts the car and we wait for the heat to kick in. We then make the ten-minute drive through town to home.

We pull into the muddy driveway. More dirt gets caked on the already filthy car.

"We really should go get it washed soon," I make this observation to Ryan who's bobbing along to the radio.

"What's the point if it's just going to get dirty again?" I stay quiet because he makes a valid point. I just like everything neat and tidy as best as it can be.

We pass by the fork in the road that would take Caitlyn to her own home. Pulling up to the front of the house, I take note of the Halloween decorations that are still up. They both glance at me in the rear-view mirror as we say "Gail" in unison.

Our mother is notorious for leaving Halloween decorations up till Christmas. She says it makes the transition of fall to winter more bearable. Caitlyn is just as annoyed by it as Ryan and I are. It at least allows us to have an inside joke.

Before the front door of the mudroom there is a doormat that says 'happiness'. We wipe our muddy shoes, head into the house, and we throw our bags down. We can see snacks awaiting us on the island.

An apple already sliced for Ryan, Triscuits and cheese spread for Caitlyn, and a granola bar for me. That's one of things we appreciate about mom's job. She works with insurance for a major company and it allows her to work from home. We all know that she's still on the clock, so we head down to the hangout space in the basement.

Caitlyn and I go directly for the pool sticks. Ryan throws himself onto the couch, stating he'll kick the winner's butt. I rack up the balls.

"Arrogant much?" I respond to his boastful comment.

"Truth hurts, Sis."

Caitlyn strikes the cue ball, sending the other balls flying in all directions. It was a good break. She's solids. On my turn I line up for the 12 ball, left pocket. I steady the pool stick on my thumb, trying to measure my force. When I am just about to send the ball rolling, my shoulder jerks. The white ball nudges forward.

"Nice one, Dufus," Ryan teases.

Trying to keep my cool I respond with an easy going, "Whatever."

Without needing to be said, I lost. And I was okay with that because I would ultimately lose to Ryan and his oversized ego. But not Caitlyn. She made him eat his words.

The two of them played a few more games before we were called up for dinner. We were having mom's famous tater tot casserole tonight.

Once seated, we bowed our heads in prayer.

 "We thank you Lord for the food we have here in front of us," Dad always leads the prayer. He has a very low, calming voice that we barely ever hear. He continues, "We ask blessings on our family and the rest of this evening." We all respond with, "Amen."

"How was everyone's day?" Mom likes hearing the recap of our day. A moment is set between the question and the answer as we swallow our food.

"My day was pretty good, Mrs. Whitten," Caitlyn is always more polite in front of authority figures. Ryan and I mock her because she knows she can address our mom as Gail at this point.

"I got a B+ on my math test, so that's good. I wasn't very confident about it, but it worked out." She goes through the rest of her day. With each subject mom is more invested. They don't break eye contact the entire time.

"Wow! What an exciting day!" Mom over exaggerates. I have a day that's reflective of Caitlyn's and mom responds less enthused.

Ryan chimes in finally, "My day was okay. Got an A on my physics test." School comes easily to Ryan. Most things do. He continues with his day from school to the extracurriculars that he's in. Mock trial goes to state next weekend. If their team wins it will mark the 30th win in a row. I'm not looking forward to this weekend as much anymore. Having him recite the same script, and my parents in a glazed-over awe, no thanks. Dad remains silent for the rest of dinner.

We all take a part in cleaning up. Us kids grab the dishes and refrigerated items while leaving the hot stuff for the adults to divide up for leftovers.

"Mrs. Whitten?" I nudge Caitlyn in the ribs and roll my eyes. She continues without correction, "Mrs. Whitten, would you mind if I stay the night?"

"Of course not! Just let your mom know," Mom welcomingly responds. The elephant in the room lingers just as heavily as its proper title. Caitlyn's parents are going through a nasty divorce and she is caught in the crossfires of it. The Whitten household is a small liberation from it.

After everything is cleaned up, we all go our different directions. Dad to his office, Mom to the living room, and the kids to their rooms, Caitlyn tagging along with me.

Once settled in downstairs we get out our homework. *English paper I'm coming for you.* I quickly reread over what I already have. I notice Caitlyn getting out her English notebook as well. *Great. Now I am sure to be distracted again. Stay focused Jenna. Just. Stay. Focused.*

"Oh, and another point I can make..." *Crap. And I don't think Mrs. Stark will take 'my friend wouldn't shut up and distracted me' as an excuse.*

I try to make my nod more annoyed at her than the topic this time. She doesn't get my social cue and continues.

"Caitlyn. Please stop. I can't focus with you talking. I'm sorry but please just stop." This time I was using the conjunction of 'but'. She humbly became quiet. "Thank you."

Adjusting my paper one more time, as if that meant I could write faster, I get started. Scribbling down the word *what*, hoping to form that into the sentence of

"What the D.A.R.E. program could do better is…" my hand loses full control.

"God dammit!" I break the snug silence.

"What? What's going on?" a frantic Caitlyn asks.

"Nothing. It's just my damn hand." That doesn't, nor should it make any sense to her. "I don't know. I've just been having these muscle spasms." I further explain. My hand shakes.

Having a bit more of an understanding she suggests an early onset of carpal tunnel. I slightly laugh, not knowing if she is joking or not. Either way, the care she is trying to show is nice.

"Can I help at all?" She offers. *Yes! God yes!*

"Yeah, sure," I respond trying to show it's not as bad as it is. The rest of the essay goes smoothly. With Caitlyn's help I get the introduction and two body paragraphs done. I should be able to get the rest of it done this weekend. I just hope that whatever the hell is going on with my hand will stop.

2.

"Please state your name."

"Carter Marcus."

"How are you employed?"

"I am a law enforcement consultant in private practice."

"How long have you been so employed?"

"Since 2011."

It's too early for this I think turning over in my bed. Ryan and Dad are already going at it with mock trial.

Caitlyn is more vocal, "Take your Law and Order episode upstairs." She throws her pillow at the door for extra effect. It works. The attorneys leave. I roll back over to see what time it is. The clock hanging on the wall reads quarter to nine. *Well I'm up.* I've always had trouble going back to sleep once awoken.

I reach for my glasses that are on my nightstand. I feel my arm move in what can only be described as slow motion. In delay from when my brain made the command, I reach my specs.

"I'm heading upstairs," I tell Sleeping Beauty who's snuggled up on the cot adjacent to my bed. A groan is her response.

In the dining room the boys occupy the table. I grab a Nutri-Grain bar from the pantry. Our kitchen is divided up into who prefers what. With the fridge centered in the middle of the back wall, the left cabinets withhold my favorite snacks, while the right cabinets belong to Ryan and his taste buds. The island bar stools are assigned seating as well. I take my place on the far left one.

"Hey kiddo, Caitlyn's still asleep?" I spin the chair in the direction of Mom's voice. I nod as I am still chewing on my breakfast. She heads over to the Keurig machine placed on the countertop. Her signature drink is a French Vanilla blend.

"Would you like some?" She asks this as a joke. Although I like the smell of coffee, I don't enjoy the taste. This has been a long-standing joke between us.

The rest of the morning is relaxing. We just got inventory for Dad's book shop so there are plenty of books to choose from. I grab a book from one of the open boxes and lie down on the couch. I get to chapter seven in *The Girl on The Train* by the time Caitlyn joins us upstairs.

"Mr. Whitten if you need help stocking, I'd be happy to." It's a nice offer Caitlyn makes, but Dad already intended for her to help. It's the family's bonding time, as he likes to call it, every Saturday. Caitlyn has been part of the family for years now. Our friendship hit the ten-year mark this past August.

Dad nods to his truck parked out front. "You can start bringing the last of the boxes out to the car." Ryan had done most of the heavy lifting. There were only a few boxes of magazines left now.

"You got it Billy Bob," Caitlyn responds eagerly. Dad's legal name is William Robert. She and my dad have a special relationship. Dad always took her under his wing like another daughter. It made up the absence of her own dad being a father figure. Caitlyn came up with that nickname the first year that she met him.

Once the truck is filled, we make the short trip over to the bookstore. We turn onto Park street and the store is the third building on the left. It's placed perfectly between a coffee shop and an antique store.

"Okay, let's do this in an orderly fashion people," Dad directs from the driver's seat before getting out.

The assembly line is Ryan, Caitlyn, Mom, me and then Dad to put the boxes exactly where he wants them.

"Mystery," Ryan starts.

"Mystery," Caitlyn continues.

"Mystery," Mom follows.

I pause with the box hanging heavy in my hands, "You'll never guess what genre, Dad."

"Mystery?" He asks as he relieves the weight from me.

"Lucky guess." I wink.

It's the last box of the last genre, Self Help, and it's handed to me. I feel secure with the weight for a brief second as it is not that heavy, but then my shoulder spasms. The box tumbles from my grip. *The Power of Now* and *Think and Grow Rich* topple out.

I try to gather them up before any dirt gets on them. I can't control my fidgeting arm and I drop them again. While kneeling I stretch my arm forward. From the corner of my eye I see dad frantically put them back in the box and closes it.

"Sorry, Dad. I don't know what's going on," I say. He shakes his head to show no worries. He's a very calm-mannered person.

"Dude, that has been going on for a few days now. You should get that checked out," Caitlyn chimes in. I rub the muscles in my right shoulder to try to get them to relax. It slowly but surely works.

"Did something happen?" Great, now Mom's worried.

"No." I reassure her, but she still insists we see a doctor on Monday. *It can't hurt* I think to myself. "Can it be during 7th hour?" I knew I wouldn't finish my English paper, so I need that extra day.

3.

"Ow! That fricken hurts man!" I shriek to the doctor who's doing my exam.

"Sorry," he voices, but doesn't change what he's doing. He continues to rotate my arms back and forth in a slow swinging motion. I can't take it anymore, and I pull back from his grip. I let my arms lie in my lap. I gingerly shrug my shoulders up and down. The tingly feeling finally eases.

"Dr. Cooper, so is this some sort of injury? Did she pull something?" My mother offers.

He pauses, "I think some tests will help determine what's going on." *This is gonna be hell.*

"Great," I say softly.

He leads us down the hall and to the left to the lab. He first orders enzyme tests. Damaged muscles release enzyme, such as creatine kinase into the blood. "We'll call you when the results are in." He tells my mother that they should be in within the next week or so. Now it's just a game of wait-and-see.

At home I research my symptoms to try and figure out what may be happening to me. I type in *arm spasms, weakness,* and *cramps in legs.* My top results are as follows: low potassium, restless leg syndrome, and Lyme disease. The last one might be possible. It is fall and I do like to go on runs.

I look further into this find. One website says that a fever, chills, muscle and joint aches, and swollen lymph nodes are all symptoms for 3-30 days after a tick bite. I feel my neck. My skin lays flat. That doesn't rule out Lyme disease though. Shooting pains, numbness, or tingling in the hands or feet for days to months after bitten. This is looking more likely. I print out this information to show Mom at dinner.

"Interesting. Well, we can bring this up to Dr. Cooper once the results are back," She comforts as she continues to set the table. I finish her task by bringing out some glasses and pouring milk into each one.

On the following Monday, a week from when I first took the tests, we get a call. While we were waiting to hear back my hands got worse. Cramping from not even doing anything has started to happen. This time Dad takes me as mom is busy with work.

Dad shakes hands with Dr. Cooper. The two of them are old friends. The friendship sparked after a girl cheated on one with the other in high school.

"So, Doc, what are we dealing with here?" Dad is never known to do small talk with serious situations. He just dives right in.

"Right, Bill the blood tests came back negative." He's speaking through a mask; his speech is muffled. "This means that we have to do further tests to determine what specific disease she has," he says as he moves each of my limbs at his own will.

I grimace at the escalating pain. I ask if it's Lyme disease. I can't focus on anything that he's saying as my discomfort grows. I pick up "nerve conduction study, spinal cord, and myopathy..." he raises my arms straight out. None of what he's saying makes sense besides knowing what my spinal cord is. "No, it's not Lyme disease but that was a valid guess." He pulls my arms forward from their sockets. I squeeze my eyes shut.

"Shall we?" Doc asks. I had completely spaced out, but I follow the social cue and stand. I follow him to another room that has a bed and a bunch of machinery next to it. I suddenly get this pit in my stomach. *This isn't going to be good.* I lie down, now in a gown and wait patiently for Dr. Cooper to get situated on his end.

"Alright Jenna, here's what's going to happen," he starts. "I am going to attach these stickers on you." He pauses to show me. "I am measuring how fast an electrical impulse moves through your nerve. This can identify nerve damage." *That doesn't sound good.* "During the test, your nerve is stimulated, usually with electrode patches attached to your skin." He points to the chords that are now attached to my body. This sounds painful. "Are you ready?" I nod. What else can I do? I can't run away. I look like a life-sized version of a marionette doll.

I feel the voltage take over my arms and then my legs. I feel a slight buzzing near each sticker on my body. My hands and knees are left shaking.

The time goes by slowly. It alternates between a minute of electricity hitting and then a minute of stimulation. This happens for easily ten minutes straight. He finally finishes with one last zap. I feel quite lethargic.

We're back in the original room. On the walls of this office are coloring pages done by children. They fill in as wallpaper. I can't decide if they are drawn by his kids or done by some of his younger patients. A family picture of the Coopers is next to this colorful art gallery.

"My kids are little Picassos, aren't they?" Well that answers that question. I try to study on something else now, in fear of hearing what Dr. Cooper might say. The pictures are no longer a choice. I focus on Doc's attire.

Besides the dead giveaway of his white coat, he has a blue sweater pulled over a white button-down. His khaki pants and nice leather shoes accessorize his look.

"The result of these tests could finally give us the answers we are looking for." He's still wearing a mask. He must be sick himself. I can hear it in his voice that he's been coughing a lot--it's scratchy and lower than normal. He continues to tell us ways to maintain these uncomfortable symptoms. Alternating heat and cold on the different areas of my body can help reduce the muscle tension. That gives me hope that my issue isn't that bad after all.

"So how did the appointment go?" Caitlyn asks handing me a shake from In and Out. She and Ryan must have gone there after school. I set the drink on the table and slurp away. I'm afraid of spilling such a tasty treat.

"It went alright, I guess. We don't have any answers yet but we're getting there." I feel the cold liquid slide down my throat. My eyes squeeze shut, and I press my tongue against the roof of my mouth.

"Brain freeze?" Ryan asks, a slight tease in his voice. I flip him off, not being able to speak yet.

"Karma's a bitch. You'll probably get one next," I say a few seconds later. Ryan smiles at this backfire. We have a good relationship as siblings. It's partially due to our closeness in age. Ironically enough he was born on August 13 and I on March 13. Mom says that's her lucky number.

Caitlyn and I go downstairs to get our homework done right away. On Monday night "The Bachelor" is on. Tonight, the bachelor is going to visit the families of the last three girls he has chosen. It's a must-see.

I pull out a scratch piece of paper to write down what I have for homework. Every school year I buy a planner and intend to be organized, but by the third week of school I lose motive.

Math 2-20 evens
Second draft for English
Worksheet for Global Studies

I pull out my math first, seeing that's my least favorite class, and I want to get it out of the way. Math has always been my worst subject. Being a junior and taking geometry shows for it. My worksheet has a bunch of different-sized circles and my task is to find the circumference of each one. Can you see why I hate it? The ten problems take me longer than I thought it would.

"Hey, can you write for me for my paper again?" I ask. I hope Caitlyn won't mind. I offer to do her social studies worksheet in return.

"I can do that first if you'd like." She likes my suggestion. It allows for her to get her Spanish homework done. It takes about 15 minutes to do my own worksheet and another five to copy the answers onto hers. Caitlyn isn't quite done, so I go upstairs to get ice packs for my hands.

When I get back, she's ready. I take out my paper and look over the suggestions Mrs. Stark made. She commented that I need a stronger conclusion paragraph. That makes sense. I did kinda give up at that point.

"Okay," I hand the essay over to her. "Let's just scrap that last paragraph and start over."

"Got it." She chalks a big X through it. The cold ice packs on my hands leave them comfortably numb, relieving any pain.

"In conclusion," I slowly start, "I believe the DARE program has its pros and cons." I pause and wait for her to write it down. I continue, "It can improve if it were to talk about these important topics to students who are already in high school as well as junior high." Caitlyn quickly jots this down. "But overall I believe the DARE program has good intentions." Still not a great conclusion, but if that's the only thing I'll get points off on, I'll still get an A. We finish just in time for the show.

"And now the final rose," the director of the show narrates, "Ashley." Nick hands her the rose, a symbol of his love, and the girls who didn't get one say their goodbyes. Nick's such an idiot. This chick is a complete bitch, yet he keeps her.

"Asshole." I nod along to Caitlyn's commentary. The show cuts to the preview of next week's episode. A helicopter ride, a walk on the beach, and a cat fight is displayed on the flat screen. Next week is the finale episode. Nick will finally propose to his final pick. It's between a rather beautiful blonde that is Ashley and a down-to-earth redhead.

Tonight, Caitlyn is expected home. This is the last night her father is in the house till he officially moves out. She doesn't seem to be too thrilled about it. I don't blame her. It puts her at a vulnerable position for a topic of argument. I take the Ranger out of the garage and drive her home.

"Hey, text me tonight if you need anything." I want to make sure she's okay. If I was allowed, I would stay the night with her.

4.

In the auditorium Mrs. Anderson, the principal, has us gathered up to see which study halls we'll be in for the grade check. The school recently started a regular and an honors study hall program. It's an incentive to keep our grades up. She calls out about 20 names for each class. I listen closely to the other names that are called along with mine.

"Nick Tilly, Cara Richardson, Noah Dund, and Charlie Reed," Mrs. Anderson finishes. I approve of all of them except for Nick. He is one of those immature guys who still whistles through pen caps.

We're excused from the auditorium and we head to our proper locations. I make my way to the English wing. Mrs. Stark is my teacher for my honors study hall. I take a seat in the second row near the door. Charlie takes a seat next to me. He and I dated for a bit last year. We mutually decided to just be friends.

"Bello," he says with a cheesy smile. That's "Charlie" talk. He's very poor in English, but he makes up for it with his fun personality.

"How are you doing?" I ask him.

"Oh, just peachy." And that's his catch phrase. He positions his head over his phone lying on the desk and cups his ears. In honors study hall we can be on our phones since our grades are C's and above.

I pull out *A Girl on the Train* from my drawstring bag. I only have a few chapters left. I must return it to Dad's inventory once I'm done. I glance over at Charlie and notice he's been staring at me.

"Good book?" he asks, his phone is still playing a YouTube video of monster trucks racing through mud. I nod, looking into his green, sparkling eyes. I identify with the character in my book. She still has love for her ex, and I would say that I would date Charlie again.

The bell rings and we exit Mrs. Stark's room. Heading down the hallway, Charlie playfully rams me into the wall. I laugh as I try to push him away.

"See ya," I say as I turn the corner, heading down for lunch. He waves as he makes his way to his favorite class, English.

Down in the cafeteria I meet Caitlyn and Ryan at a round table near the windows. Today's options for lunch are cereal bar or hamburgers.

"So, which will it be ladies? Slaughtered cow or yummy cereal?" Ryan's a vegetarian, but he knows I can't stand cereal. They go for the gross crunchy stuff while I help myself to some protein. In line I stand behind a guy whose hair is long enough to be put into a man bun. That seems to be the trend these days. Half of the male population at Valley High are into it.

Once we fill up our trays, we have to punch our school code to pay for our food. I hold my blue plastic plate with one hand. I type in 20396, about to punch in the seven to finish my code when I spastically throw my tray forward.

"Shit!!" I don't know if I'm screaming about the mess or the shooting pain in my left arm. The lunch lady bends down to clean it up. I crouch as well, but the pain won't stop.

 I take napkins to sop up the peaches and their juices. My appetite has all together gone away. Once everything is cleaned up, I grab the still intact milk and take my seat.

"Nice one there, Spaz." I am not in the mood for Ryan's sarcasm. He reads my facial expressions and cuts it out. Apologizing he offers me the bag of chips he bought with his lunch.

I say, "No thanks." I feel my back pocket vibrate. It's mom. She's going to pick me up in ten minutes for an appointment. My test results must be in.

Lunch just finishes when mom arrives. I exit the school doors to go to her blue minivan. It's a pretty nice day out in Valley City. The clouds look like a kid's drawing where they turned the crayon sideways and scribbled away. Mom smiles nervously. We are both anxious about the results.

We get to the Aspirus clinic. It's a good 15-minute wait before a nurse calls us back. My 5'4" frame has lost weight. The scale reads 107. That's down eight pounds. The nurse leads us to Dr. Cooper's familiar room. The nurse comments that she'll make the doctor aware of my unintentional weight loss. After vitals are taken Dr. Cooper comes in.

"How are we doing today, ladies?" he asks with forced enthusiasm.

"We're fine, thanks" *We're not fine*. "Yourself?" Still keeping up the act he says he's doing well. Today he's wearing a burgundy sweater vest and a white button-down. *What's up with doctors and layers?* It works for his thin body type though. I feel my palms sweat as I wait for him to say what's going on.

"So...with the tests we took we were looking for anything other than what it is. And since you've lost weight it confirms the results even more." *What the hell does that mean?* My mom grabs hold of my hand, as if to emotionally stabilize herself. My own hands are trembling.

"With ruling everything else out… it appears you have amyotrophic lateral sclerosis, or ALS." There are so many questions, but the shock of it all leaves my mind blank. All I can do is shake my head back and forth. Mom speaks up.

"So, what does that mean?" Her voice is faint. I'm not sure she actually wants the answer to that question.

Squirming in his chair, "It takes over her control for voluntary muscle movements. That includes chewing and talking." The air around us becomes stale.

"But there's a cure, right? She can get better, can't she?" Mom is frantically hopeful.

"Gail...no...it's a progressive disease." He wishes that's all there was to say, but he continues, "If she's lucky she has three to five years." This makes mom cry. My body trembles but my brain is still. *If I'm lucky?* Dr. Cooper gives us some pamphlets of information and schedules another appointment for us to come back in another two weeks. We stand to leave this heady room.

"And Gail I put some references in for counseling. I think that would be a good idea."

"Yes, of course. Thank you."

The car ride home is quiet. Mom is trying to hold herself together. One of her hands is on the steering wheel while the other is glued to my hand. I still don't know what to think about it. You know how people say we're all dying? Well, I feel like I'm on death row.

My hourglass just flipped.

We get home and everyone has questions. I want to be alone. I want this day to be over. Mom makes her way to a living room chair. Everyone follows and places themselves on the couch or floor. I sit in the other tan recliner.

"Gail?" Dad tries to break mom's deer-in-headlights trance. "What does she have?"

She opens her mouth to speak but she just inhales deeply. With the exhale, tears roll down her cheeks.

"I have ALS." The words didn't feel right coming out of my mouth, but that's what was confirmed. Ryan stands, his hairy ankles becoming bare from his too-short of jeans. He doesn't know who to comfort--his bawling mother or his sick but rather quiet sister. Dad allows his wife to sob into his dress pants, as he stands next to her, rubbing her back.

"Alright, so where do we go next?" Dad is still composed.

"Nowhere." My first emotion is anger. I have been calm, but now as dad wants to fix the inevitable, I become angry.

"There is no getting better." I stare past everyone and look at the fireplace that's on. The lively flames flicker. I stand up and pull the switch down to turn it off, a sense of control.

"Dr. Cooper said I have three to five years." Saying my life span brings forth tears. Ryan steps over Caitlyn to get to me. He pulls me in close to his chest. I feel Caitlyn's long fingernails rub my back in a soothing motion. I pull away from him.

"I'm sorry." My voice is shaky. Ryan pulls me back in and lets me just cry. He's a good big brother. I then feel his own tears fall from his six-foot figure. Everyone at this point has taken their turn at shedding tears.

"So, what's for dinner? I think some comfort food is badly needed." I break the cry fest. Everyone laughs in relief.

The rest of the evening goes well. We act like it's just another night. Dad makes commentary on the dish.

"You can make dinner tomorrow night if all you're going to do is complain." Mom jabs. Dad shuts up.

5.

The next morning mom insists that I stay home and not push myself. I tell her that I still want to go to school.

"Okay, but if you want to come home just text me," she says gently.

I ride shotgun on the way to school. I watch Ryan drive with extreme caution. He stays below the speed limit and takes turns at a snail's pace.

"If ALS doesn't kill me, your slow driving will."

He sped up after that. I don't want to be treated like I'm fragile. My muscles are deteriorating, yes. But right now, I can handle a brake check here or there.

We park in the leaf-covered parking lot. I wait to unbuckle.

"Hey guys. Can we not say anything about..." the words are still hard to get out "...about you know?" They understand and agree right away.

Walking the halls of the school feels different now. Everything around me feels alive while I just feel like I'm existing, not alive but just here. I fake smile at familiar faces.

People say you'll never see anyone after you graduate, but that isn't supposed to be due to death. There will be no ten-year reunion, seeing former friends' lives on Facebook, or looking at cop reports to see your kindergarten sweetheart wound up in jail. My name will be in the obituaries and people will say, "She died so young."

I log onto my computer and look at my grades. They read A's all the way down. I pride myself in being a good student, but now I wonder what's the point?

During study hall I pull out my homework but have no motivation to do it. Charlie has his head over his phone again. I don't even have an interest in pulling out my own phone. I lay my head on my desk.

"Hey you doing okay?" Charlie nudges my arm. I turn to his direction. I shake my head yes. I don't feel like talking.

"Come on. Cheer up!" He pauses his video on his phone and continues, "Life ain't that bad." I smile faintly. I appreciate him trying to make me feel better, but he has no idea. I take a nap for the rest of the hour. The bell rings finally and I stand to leave.

"Hey Jenna, have a second?" Mrs. Stark asks from her desk. I walk over to her. My ankles feel stiff. "Are you doing okay? You seem off." *I am off. My body's killing me.*

"I'm fine. Just tired I guess." I really don't want to talk about it with anyone. She lets it go and wishes me a good day.

Down in the lunchroom I don't bother to get food. I think about texting Mom to come get me. Ryan and Caitlyn sit on either side of me. Our table is filled with gloom.

"So, you doing okay, Sis?" Ryan asks softly. I'm honest with him. I tell him I feel drained, that I want to go home.

"Well, I can run you back quickly. We have time." He's a senior so he has the right of passage to leave the building during lunch. Nobody would notice if I were to go with him. I ponder this for a second. I turn it down. I'll probably be missing a lot of school in the future, so I'll just tough it out.

English comes soon enough. It's my favorite class even though lately it's been giving me a hard time with all the writing. I try to seem more peppy so Mrs. Stark doesn't pull me aside again.

Today she tells us that our next essay is relating something concrete to something abstract. I choose water and hopelessness. I feel someone's presence looking over my shoulder. It's Mrs. Stark.

"Hopelessness?" She doesn't say anything else. She just evolves into someone else's shadow. I sink back in my desk. *Well, it's how I feel.* I catch Caitlyn peering at me. I feel her disappointment. The second stage of grief hits me again. I feel enraged. Pounding my fist on the desk I leave the classroom.

Fuck off. I just want everyone to fuck off. I'm pacing the hallway. My body temperature seems to be escalating. *I'm not sick. I'm fucking fine.* Clenching my jaw so tight gives me a headache.

With my back up against the wall I slide down to the floor. I close my eyes. *Breathe Jenna. Just breathe.* I hear a door open. With my eyes still closed, I hear a kid get a drink of water. I keep still.

"Jenna, you alright?" The voice is low. It's a kind of voice that speaks with the back of the throat. It's Charlie. He takes a seat next to me. He knocks his knee into mine. I lift my head.

"Yep. Just peachy." The response brings forth tears. I let my head fall into his green hooded shoulder. I appreciate him just letting me cry. He doesn't push for a conversation to happen. He just lets me cry.

I meet Ryan and Caitlyn at the usual spot. My face must still be red, because they rush towards me.

"I'm fine you guys. I promise." I don't want to worry them. And I really am doing better. Caitlyn suggests for me ride shotgun on the way home. Usually we switch between morning and after school. I turn the offer down. I don't want to be treated differently.

When we get home, Mom is standing outside the main entrance. She waves at us as we pull into the garage. She must have raced right over to the mudroom cause she greets us there as well.

"How was your day?" She isn't asking everyone. The question is directed at me. I feel like such an attention whore.

"My day was fine." This answer isn't detailed enough for her. She goes through my entire schedule and asks about each class. I didn't think she knew my day that well. When she reaches English, I hesitate in response.

"It was fine. Just like all the others." She doesn't buy it.

"Oh honey." She pulls me in for a hug.

My voice muffled from her shirt I croak out the words, "I'm fine."

Dad comes home early from work. He claims nobody was going to come into the store anyway due to it being a Wednesday, but I know that it's not true. I wish everything wasn't suddenly revolved around me. I feel like such a bother.

6.

The calendar on my phone reads Thursday, October 19th. It's been exactly a week since I was diagnosed. I have my first appointment with a therapist today. Mom tells me her name is Lynelle and that she's in her early 40s. I feel optimistic about this meeting. It's this lady's job to listen to me. I don't feel like I am taking time away from her day. I have a set time to talk and hopefully it will quiet down the concern at home.

Lynelle's office is very cliché. There's a couch and a chair directly across from it with a rocker next to that. I pull the washed-out maroon pillow, which matches the sofa, over to be used for a back rest. I don't want to lie down so I sit. Lynelle claims the rocker leaving Mom the chair.

"So, Jenna, can you give me an update as to where you are in all of this?" Her voice is nasally but not in an annoying way. It gives her character.

"Well, next week I have an appointment with Dr. Cooper." She jots that down on her yellow sketchpad. She doesn't break eye contact though. I explain how this all started in my arms. I tell her about the muscle cramps and the incident in the lunchroom.

"Mmhm. And how's your mood been through each of these episodes?"

I guess I waited too long with a response cause Mom jumps in. "I think she's had some spouts of anger, but really the concern is the depression that she's falling into."

Lynelle doesn't look at my mother. She's making me feel like I am the patient, not Mom. I appreciate that.

"Jenna, do you think you've fallen into a depression?" she asks this in such a gentle voice. *How can I not be? I'm losing the ability to move.*

"I guess." I don't know why I am feeling the need to be strong. Maybe it's because Mom isn't able to be right now, but I explain my lack of interest in school. Lynelle nods along as I tell her I still am in disbelief about all of this. I don't understand why this is happening to me.

"Have you done research on ALS?" she asks.

"Not a lot. I guess I haven't been emotionally ready to do so." She is so understanding of this. Lynelle tells me that she thinks it will behoove me to do so.

"Maybe you can do that as a family," she suggests to Mom.

"Absolutely. Bill and I have ordered some books on ALS to learn more." I'm sure that means they bought several copies to sell some in the store. Might as well make some profit off this damn disease.

The session ends. I have another appointment for the following week on Wednesday.

At home Caitlyn and Ryan are playing Grand Theft Auto on the Xbox downstairs.

"Here. Go steal that firetruck." Ryan hands me the controller. In the game you can hijack people's vehicles and run the person over from whom you stole it.

My character was a guy dressed in camo attire. I was known to be a pretty good driver in the game. It goes steady for a bit. I make the turns while going at full speed. I race in between traffic. My hand starts tingling. While driving on a straight stretch I take time to shake the pain out.

"Jenna, you're like Fast and Furious!" Caitlyn cheers. My thumb on the joystick twitches. I run over a pedestrian.

"Dammit." I curse. Cops are now on my back end. I toss the controller over to Ryan. I can't play anymore. My hand is cramping too badly. I press my thumb into my right palm. I massage the muscles out.

"I'm gonna go for a run." I tell the two gamers. I change into a pair of blue shorts and a purple volleyball t-shirt. Skipping up the stairs to the kitchen I feel my calves ache.

I slip on my sneakers and head out the door. It's another nice day out. There is a light breeze, and the sun is making the descent to set. I start running down the driveway. I feel alive. The trees are vibrant with different colors. I feel the blood pumping through my veins. I inhale as my left heel hits the pavement and exhale as my right toe touches down. The air feels warm in my throat. I love it.

I go a mile and a half and make it to the stop sign near the highway. I turn around. The silhouettes of the trees and nature are beautiful. The sky has highlighter orange and pink streaks through it. I feel calm.

I have about a quarter mile to go before I reach home. I'm going at a steady pace. My legs are starting to feel sore. *The faster you go the quicker you'll be home. Just push through it.* The pep talk doesn't help. My legs feel like stretched out rubber.

My pace is getting harder to maintain. As I push myself forward, I feel my leg give out below me. My muscle just snaps underneath me. I fall and my knee scrapes the pavement. Blood trickles into my sock.

 I can see the outline of our house in the near distance. I limp up the driveway. The orange and pink colors of the sky smear together into a washed-out magenta.

My tennis shoe rubs against the back of my ankle. I feel the skin underneath my scrunched sock become raw. My knee stings in the fresh open air. I reach home by the time the blood dries.

"Mom?" I push the door open. She comes over in a hurry.

"What happened? You shouldn't have been out there by yourself." She's right, but I haven't really experienced any leg issues yet. My hands have just been the problem.

"My leg felt stiff, and then I fell," I explain as I wipe the blood with a Kleenex. My muscles feel like a tight rubber band.

She leads me to the couch. I slowly fall back into the cushions. Mom props my leg on a stool and bandages the wound.

"We need to bring this up to Dr. Cooper," Mom says. I focus on her appearance to soften her tone. She and I look a lot alike. We both have rich brown hair except mine is down to my breasts whereas she keeps hers just above her shoulders. Her eyes are the same clear blue shade as mine. I wonder how this new ailment will affect me further.

7.

Caitlyn's mom invites me over for dinner the next night. I haven't been over to their house in a while. We're used to going to mine.

"So, Jenna how have you been feeling?" Kathy is acting like I have a cold, not a major degenerative disease. In the prior few months before the divorce everyone's title changed to just their name. Mr. Briston became Jim and Mrs. became Kathy.

"Good. School's keeping me on my toes." *Toes that cramp from standing up for five minutes.*

I take a seat at the dinner table. Kathy has definitely been physically affected by her divorce. Her once-slim body has filled out and her attire changed from fashion forward outfits to blue jeans and a paint stained t-shirt.

"And yourself?" I return the rhetorical question. We both know the other has been not great, but society tells us to ask the faded question and return it with a deceptive response. She follows the social cue.

"I'm doing well, Dear." Her cooking has also been affected. She brings out a pot of box-made mac 'n cheese. She dips in the wooden spoon and scoops out a hefty serving for each of us. I get up from the table.

"Oh, what do you need? I'll grab it." Caitlyn isn't showing a normal level of politeness. She's trying to cater to my illness.

"Just ketchup. It's alright. I've got it." I shuffle past her. I grab the bottle from the fridge and come back. I drown my noodles in the red condiment. Kathy makes a face.

"Hey, don't knock it till you try it." I think ketchup adds flavor. I'm one of the few with this opinion.

The house feels weird without Jim. He isn't a bad guy. He's just is a workaholic. More dedicated to the stock market than his wife.

I'm allowed to stay the night, but I haven't felt comfortable with sleepovers since I've been diagnosed. Usually I would just walk home and cut through the woods as a shortcut but now I'm worried my legs might fail me again. Caitlyn grabs her mom's keys and drives me back.

"Thanks. I'll see you later." It's close to 8:30 by the time I get home. Normally it wouldn't be a big deal to come home at this hour on a school night, but tonight mom wigs out.

"Where the hell have you been?" she demands. She knows I was at Caitlyn's, but the scolding doesn't stop.

"I was worried sick! With your condition you can't be out so late!"

Dad comes up behind her. He just got back from the store. He was making orders. "Honey, what's going on?" He puts his hand on the small of her back. She calms down a bit. Dad's my constant hero. He's the calm in the storm.

"I know she was at Caitlyn's, but now with everything I don't want her out so late."

Dad nods along. He knows she's overreacting, but he lets her talk.

"I'm upset because I care. If I didn't care I wouldn't be mad right now." Mom shows her love in an odd way, but it still is appreciated.

The argument finally dies down, and I head to my room. The constant aching in my body leaves me exhausted. Sleep is like my restart button, allowing me to tackle the next day.

8

There's a meeting scheduled for 7:30 with Mrs. Anderson, the nurse, and the guidance counselor. We're going to tell them about my condition. I feel nervous. My parents and I enter the conference room. Everyone is already seated around the large table.

Dad starts the conversation. "Last week we found out Jenna has ALS." Dad dressed like his usual self, in a flannel tucked into blue jeans, while mom is wearing a nice pants suit as if she's my attorney. Everyone is quiet. They were expecting to hear I had a stomach bug or the usual flu, not a serious disease.

Mr. Porter, the guidance counselor, is the first to speak. "We need to rethink classes and graduation then." My parents seem to be disappointed with this response. They are more worried about accommodating to my physical needs, not my academic progress.

"Mr. Porter, grades are not our main concern," Mom quickly replies. Mom continues to explain how this disease will slowly debilitate me. I'm uncomfortable.

"Sooner or later she will be in a wheelchair. Will the school be able to assist to this?" Dad has spoken up now. I hadn't thought of that. My legs just began to bother me, but I hadn't thought that maybe within a few months I'll be wheelchair bound.

"There are elevators," I tell them. I don't want to feel like we're interrogating them. Mrs. Anderson seems to be relieved by this comment.

"Yes. And we can move her classes to the main level," Mr. Porter, rightfully so by his job description, is still wanting to discuss scheduling. At the end of the meeting we finally get to it. They printed out my new schedule. It reads: band, chemistry, math, study hall, lunch, and English in the library. This schedule will be implemented once I am unable to walk the stairs.

"Where were you this morning?" Charlie asks in study hall. We also have chemistry together. I still haven't told him. I don't know how to. I'm afraid he'll also treat me different. That's the last thing I want.

"I'm a rebel. I skipped."

He gasps.

"How dare you!" I laugh at his shock. I want to keep the conversation light and fun. I ask him if we can hang out after school.

"I need to tell you something." He needs to know. It doesn't feel right keeping this secret from him. He says we'll go for a drive.

After school he pulls up in his white, beaten up, pickup truck. I push myself up into his cab with my left leg, my good leg. Peace Tea cans litter his front dash. I'm not surprised. That drink seems to be his vice.

"So, where we heading?" He asks. I tell him he's the driver so wherever. He guns it. I wasn't prepared and I grab hold of the passenger handle. I don't even have my seat belt on yet. He smiles proudly.

"Cause I'm T.N.T., I'm dynamite," he's singing badly off key. He cranks up the volume even more. He loves ACDC. The speakers next to my feet vibrate with the booming bass. He drives wildly around turns and speeds up hills. Soaring down the hills make my stomach lift and I laugh. There's never a dull moment with Charlie.

"Can we talk?" I ask once his song finishes. His turning of the dial down signals yes.

"Ummm, so I have news."

"Good or bad?" He fires back. *Shit.*

I hesitate. I can't lie to him. "Bad." This causes his to pull over. We now sit in silence in a dugout near the road. He keeps the car running. The humming of the engine fills in for background noise.

"For the past month I've been having different issues and we went to the doctor."

"You're pregnant," he interrupts. *God dammit, Charlie.* "And I'm the unwilling essence you've stolen." Now he's joking. We fooled around before, but we never had sex.

"Shut up. This is serious." I secretly appreciate his witty remark. I continue. "I have been having *muscle* issues," I tell him. He seems to be understanding.

"Yeah, the hand thing you've been doing." He's referring to my twitching thumb at random times. I nod to his observation. "So, what do you have?" He's fully realizing the seriousness of this situation.

"ALS," I say not looking at him. He turns back to face the steering wheel. I can't scan how he's feeling. *Does he know what that is? Is he clueless? Is he upset?* He pulls the gear back into drive.

"How long you got?" His voice goes back to the springy happiness I'm used to. *Thank you, God.*

"I don't know how long you're stuck with me so you better treat me well." I know he's okay. I want to show him that I am also okay.

We continue our drive on the countryside. I roll down my window and rest my head. I love the wind going through my hair. I close my eyes. He puts on my favorite song. The wise words of Lennon Cohen's "Hallelujah" plays through the radio.

9.

Mom and Dad both attend my appointment with Dr. Cooper. Mom brings a notepad with an update scribbled down on it. We want to make sure to tell him about my leg symptoms.

"How's everybody doing?" Dr. Cooper walks in. Today he has chosen a purple sweater with the usual white button down. Dad stands to shake hands with him. Dr. Cooper does the regular checkup steps including taking my blood pressure and pulse. He asks me to sit up on the sterile table.

"And breathe in," he directs me. He puts the head of his stethoscope up to my chest. He asks how the symptoms in my hands have been.

Mom answers for me. "They have been about the same, but our concern right now are her legs. She has been complaining about cramps in her feet and stiffness in her calves. She had a fall from these symptoms" Doc goes to the end of the bed. He pushes my feet towards me and waits for my reaction. My leg jerks back into my chest. I attend to the shooting pain by caressing the specific areas.

"This is normal with this disease." He's making this statement like it's a good thing. I want to leave. My anxiety is climbing. He doesn't help. "Within the next few months I suspect you will need assistance to walk." *Seriously?* "That's not to say a wheelchair but maybe a cane or walker." I want to cry. These are facts, not mean stated opinions.

Dr. Cooper sets up an appointment with a physical therapist. We are to meet with Ashley on Friday, but for now he prescribes vitamins and muscle relaxers. I am to take a zinc supplement to help protect my immune system. Doc doesn't want me at any risk of being sick on top of everything else.

10.

The physical therapy building is located near Golden Harvest, our local fresh organic store. I'm surprised the street they are both located on isn't call Health Avenue.

Mom joins me for this first appointment. We are greeted by a lady with light brown, wavy hair. She introduces herself as Ashley. She's wearing black jeans with brown boots and a beige sweater. Her appearance is very earth toned.

"Hi, Jenna. Nice to meet you," she warmly greets. She has me stand on a scale and takes my height. I feel fatigued. We walk to her office. In there, there are a bunch of posters pinned up. One is a diagram of the human muscles and another of the skeleton.

She explains at this appointment we'll be discussing exercises I can do at home to stretch out my muscles. She gets out a lime green stretch band with black handles. She wants me to stretch each leg for a minute straight. For my hands she wants me to use a pen or a pencil and lay it flat on a desk and roll my palm over it.

Ashley did her own research on my illness. She printed out information. She hands me a small packet. On the top of one page it reads "The Different Stages of ALS." I get nervous. My future inabilities lie neatly in my hands. I file through the papers and read "Patient will need personal assistance within months of diagnosis." I feel overwhelmed by it all.

"Thanks for the info. We appreciate it," Mom says in a cheerful tone.

On our drive home I notice the change in weather as the once bright leaves are now dull and fall to the ground. Pretty soon winter will be here. Most people in our small town of Valley City find winter long and unbearable. I am usually part of the minority who loves the white dustings of snow and enjoys snowshoeing and skiing. I feel saddened that this year will be different. As I think about what I will miss out on my sorrow grows.

11.

Sure enough the end of November flies by with many appointments of therapy, checkups with Dr. Cooper and physical therapy. December arrives and winter is in full effect. Dad calls for a family meeting.

"We need to discuss the inevitable. Which is having an in-home nurse," he starts. He goes on to explain he will be working in the store seven days a week instead of six.

"And I asked for more hours as well." This is mom who takes over the conversation. "I will be traveling to other counties to work with insurance." She sounds unexcited about it all.

"We need the money with everything that is going on," Dad states. It's true, but it makes me feel like such a problem. They tell me that we will be interviewing people to potentially be an in-home nurse. One lady is scheduled for tomorrow and an older woman the next.

A middle-aged woman walks up the walkway to our house. She plays with her shirt, yanking it down over her skirt. She seems nervous. Without even being introduced to her I'm thinking she won't be a good fit.

Dad's tall stature seems to intimidate her more. She stutters as she introduces herself. Her name is Sara. We welcome her into our house and begin with the interview.

"What's your prior experience?" Mom asks.

"Well...um...actually…" I'm already disinterested as she tells us this would be her first job, but she up for a challenge. I don't want to be seen as a challenge. Dad senses my attitude toward her and cuts the interview short. Sara acted like she was trying to fix some sort of mid-life crisis and caring for another human was it. Well, not me.

Nancy is the second person we interviewed. She was a short lady. She looked to be in her late 60s. She had grey, short hair and walked slouched over. It seemed as if she herself would soon need some kind of care. This interview lasted shorter than the first.

Then a woman with highlighted blonde hair who looks to be in her late 20s enters our home. She's dressed nicely in a floral shirt with a cardigan pulled over.

"Hi. Mr. Whitten I'm Tess," she introduces herself. Dad seems to be impressed with how this young woman is displaying herself. We take a seat at the dining room table.

"May I see your resume?" Mom asks. Tess hands over a stapled packet of papers. Now I'm impressed. She has experience working at Friendly Village which is our local nursing home. She shares how her mother was diagnosed with MS and she was her first patient.

"Wonderful, I would love to meet her sometime. Maybe she and Jenna could talk," Mom pipes in. There's an uncomfortable silence.

"She passed away last year." Mom gives her her condolences. "I have stayed with that nursing home though, but I'm looking for that more personalized care again."

The interview lasted about ten more minutes before we lead her out. She drives away in her blue Mini Cooper. We all gather in the kitchen. Pulling out a bag of pretzels, Dad asked what we thought.

"I liked her," Mom starts. I agree. She was nice and didn't seem like she would be condescending and talk to my illness and not me. I pop one of the pretzels into my mouth. I slowly chew on the snack. It gets stuck in my teeth.

"So, is she the one?" Tess was a good fit. She had a good head on her shoulders and was personable.

We decided we would call her tonight to give her the news.

"Tess, hi. It's Mrs. Whitten calling. How are you?"

"I'm doing well. Yourself? How's Jenna?" The phone is set on speaker phone.

"I'm good." I respond from the other end of the table.

I'm the one to tell her she got the job. Tess give us her thanks with enthusiasm. She is scheduled to come tomorrow at 7:00. She is to come in as Mom and Dad both leave for work, and she stays through dinner.

I call Caitlyn that night. "She seems to be pretty cool. I don't know too much about her but still." My voice is excited. I kinda look at this as gaining another friend. My circle is small. It involves Caitlyn, Charlie, and Ryan. Pretty sad actually. I tell Caitlyn she'll meet Tess tomorrow.

"Awesome." We hang up. I know this new edition to my support group will be good.

I set my alarm clock for 30 minutes earlier than I normally do. I want to be awake for when Tess arrives. I also want to show her what I'm still capable of.

12.

I wake up at 6:30 the next morning. A list of my routine goes through my mind: I need to take a shower, do my hair, and get dressed before 7:00. I pick out a pair of blue jeans, ones that aren't too tight to get on and a Valley High sweatshirt. My legs feel really stiff this morning. I take my elastic band with me to stretch them out.

I pass by Ryan's room. He always sleeps with his door open, whereas I like mine closed. I see a groggy version of him roll over. The lights must have bothered him, but hey that's his own fault.

Once in the bathroom, I undress. The mirror reflects a gangly looking girl with a flat chest. *No wonder why you're single.* I turn the water on for the shower.

While waiting for it to warm up I do my stretches. I lay my leg out straight with the band around my foot and flex my ankle forward. I hold it for a minute and do the same to the other leg. I notice that afterward my legs feel wobbly. I push the knob on top of the bath faucet down and get in. The idea of falling in the shower makes me worrisome.

I let the hot water rush through my hair. It feels so relaxing, but I can't waste time for pleasure. I quickly shampoo and condition my hair. The bathroom clock reads 6:45 when I get out. I pat down my body with the available blue towel. *Ryan, you're not gonna like this.* I turn my hair dryer on. His bedroom is right next to our bathroom. *Sorry, Bro.* As my thin and fine hair dries its color becomes lighter.

I sit on top of of the sink counter to give my legs a break. I let them swing gently. It's 6:55 when my hair is completely dry. Now it's the task of getting dressed. Lately that's been more of a struggle, but I want to show I can still do it.

Now with my leg issues balance has been a problem. I need to sit down to put my pants on. The bathroom tiles are cold on my thighs. I scrunch up one pant leg and stick my foot through. I squirm to get them up the rest of the way.

Now for the hardest part. My bra. My forearms are pulsing as I strain them behind my back. My fingers cramp as I try to grip the plastic hooks. I close my eyes in prayer to get it to clasp together on my first try. *God is good, Ladies and Gentlemen.*

I hear a higher woman's voice upstairs. Tess must be here. I clumsily run up the stairs to greet her.

"Hi Tess, you're here already?" I ask looking down at an imaginary wristwatch. She cracks a smile. My parents give me a hug as they head out to work. Now it's just me and Tess.

"Ryan should be up shortly," I break the silence. Today she's wearing gray pants with a sky-blue button up. I feel bad that I don't have anything for her to help with. I didn't let her do her job.

"So, I need to take my meds in the morning. I can show you that." She likes my idea. I pull open a draw next to the garbage in the kitchen. I take out four orange transparent containers. I hand them over to her to look at the labels.

"Okay it looks like you have a supplement for zinc, vitamin D, Baclofen, and Sertraline," Tess confirms. The last two were a muscle relaxer and an antidepressant. She shakes her head in understanding. She hands over a white pill cap with all the meds in it.

"If you ever need to talk, I'm here for you," she offers. Before I give a response, Ryan dramatically enters.

"Sup ladies?" he says to swoon. *God Ryan this is not a hookup for you.* I roll my eyes.

"Ryan, you're on your own for school. Tess and I are picking up Caitlyn." *Sorry for the cock block.*

Tess's Mini Cooper is smaller than I anticipated. I bring my chair all the way forward to leave room for Caitlyn and her long legs. When we arrive at her house Caitlyn is already standing outside waiting for us.

"Hey, dude, nice ride," Caitlyn compliments Tess. She gets in the back seat.

"Caitlyn this is Tess. She's gonna tag along with us today," I introduce them. Tess is scheduled to join me in all my classes and assist me if I need help.

13.

My first class of the day is band. Conveniently enough so is Ryan and Caitlyn's. I get out my alto sax and pep band music. Tonight, we are playing for a boys' basketball game. Ryan is already seated with his trumpet. Caitlyn is still putting her clarinet together. Our band teacher, Mrs. P. starts us off with a roll off as we play our school song. I look up from the music and see Tess bobbing along to the music. I grin from under my reed.

"I remember when I was in band," Tess tells us as we head for our next class.

"Oh yeah? What instrument?" Caitlyn asks. Tess says she played flute through high school and even college. I like learning more about her. It makes me feel like this is more of a friendship, not a patient-care taker relationship.

Charlie comes in late to chemistry. He looks stressed.

"What's up?" I ask him as he takes his seat.

He's panting "My truck broke down." I'm surprised this didn't happen sooner. "I had to run here from the auto center." That's a few blocks away.

Mr. Vaughn interrupts our conversation by handing out our instructions for the lab. Charlie and I partner up. The lab is to burn different substances and guess what they are based on the color of the flame.

We head for the back-lab bench. Tess tags along.

"So, you're the assistant," Charlie comments. Kinda caught off guard she nods her head.

"Yes, well kind of. I'm a caretaker. My name's Tess." I feel bad for not doing a proper introduction. Mr. Vaughn is going around handing out fire starters. When he gets to our table he hesitates.

"I'll do it." I put out my hand for the metal device. His facial expressions show that he is unsure about this idea. He glances over at Tess. She gives him the nod of approval. *Don't fail me now hands.* Charlie gives me a thumbs up.

It's a team effort to get the flame lit. He works the gas from the Bunsen burner while I flick the fire starter. My left hand starts to cramp as I squeeze the metal striker together. A spark hits my fingers and I drop it.

"Shit," I curse, rubbing my burn.

"Are you okay?" They both ask at the same time. I nod my head yes and run it under the sink that is conveniently there. I let Tess light it. This incident makes me feel embarrassed.

At each class, Tess introduces herself to the teacher and then takes a quiet seat in the back. I find myself looking over my shoulder at her. I don't know if it's to reassure myself or to make her feel valuable. Either way she smiles back each time.

Lunch finally comes and the gang and I take our spots. Tess sits across from us at the empty semicircle. I can tell she is trying to be invisible and just be present when I need her. I want her to feel comfortable enough to engage, to join our small group of weirdos.

I feel someone tap me on the head. A tall kid in a camouflage sweatshirt passes by me. He turns around and gives a wide grin. It's Charlie. I can't help but laugh at his tease.

After lunch I have two classes, phys. ed. and English.

"So, you need help in there?" Tess asks as we stand outside of the changing room. I feel embarrassed. The thought of her helping me get changed at school hadn't crossed my mind before. I feel my cheeks get red.

"I think I'm good." I was the last one out from the changing room, but I'd rather have that than the full embarrassment. When I get out the kids are already playing dodgeball. I pick a team and join. Following the rules from the movie *Dodgeball,* I excel in the game: dodge, duck, dip, dive, and dodge, I make it pretty far before getting out. I take a seat on the floor by the closed-up bleachers.

"You doing alright?" Tess asks. I'm panting but smile to show I'm fine. She takes a seat next to me and hands me my water bottle. The cold water feels nice in my overheated throat. I hold the metal bottle up to my forehead. It cools me down a bit. My legs are throbbing in pain. I stretch and touch my toes. My calves feel like they are going to snap.

A few moments later the other kids gather the balls and go to change. *Ugh I don't want to get up.* Careful what you wish for. I make the command to stand, but my legs lay horizontal on the floor. Tess puts a hand out. I take hold, but I soon realize that won't be enough. I don't have the strength to pick myself up. Noticing this she crouches down and places my arms around her neck. Using her knees, she lifts me up to a standing position.

"You okay?" She asks as she leads us into the locker room. I leave this question unanswered. *I don't know.* The other kids hurry up to change as they see Tess assist me. I keep my eyes on the tile floor. Making eye contact with anyone will make me susceptible to their pity. Tess waits till it's just us in the locker room. She sits me on the bench placed in the middle of each set of lockers.

In silence she removes my white cross-country shirt. I regret changing into a sports bra at the beginning of class. She sets my regular bra in my lap as she pulls my sports bra over my head. I close my eyes. *Don't you dare cry, Jenna.* The embarrassment is too much, and I feel tears slowly roll down my cheeks. She changes me into my baggy sweatshirt before she asks if I'm okay.

"Um... yeah," I croak out. The tears pour more as she removes my pants. The nylon shorts slip off easily and expose my underwear covered bottom. Tess uses my method of scrunching up the pant legs before fitting my feet into them.

"Ready?" she asks a silent me before hoisting me up again. I lean heavily on her as she pulls my jeans over my thighs and up my hips. When she's done, she takes a seat next to me. She puts a hand on my shoulder.

"Jenna, I am so sorry you have to go through this. Please know I am wanting to help you in the most comfortable way possible." I sniffle to her kindness. She hands me some toilet paper before we head to English class.

In Mrs. Starks' room, Tess pulls her aside and explains why we're late. Mrs. Stark looks up from their conversation and makes eye contact with me. She smiles in pity. I look down at my desk. *This isn't going to be your last hard day, Jenna. Get over it.* I take a deep breath in and look up, ready to engage with the world.

"Hey wanna go for a drive after school?" I smile at Caitlyn's offer. I knew what this meant, a long drive while blasting music from the car's speakers. I text Ryan to tell him our plans. This is his response: *Finally letting me have some alone time with Tess?*

"Hey Tess, wanna join us in a car ride?" I ask. She says that sounds fun. *Nope* I text back.

We meet Ryan at home to drop the Mini Cooper off and us girls take the Audi. I doubt myself with driving just as much as they do so we let Caitlyn have the wheel.

She drives the speed limit on the highway, but once on backroads she guns it. I lean my chair back. With the soft acoustic song of "American Pie" playing through the speaker, I close my eyes.

"This is why we're friends Caitlyn," I shout over the music. "You drive me around and it's nice." Her speed slows.

"I'm your Uber!" She exclaims. Tess and I burst out laughing.

"No! Not like that!" I say, but she won't let it go. The rest of the car ride I lie back and relax, letting the music fill the air around me.

We head home when we get a text from Ryan saying we have to head for pep band. On our ride back the sky is a dark navy color. Black figures of trees stand out against the evening sky. When we get home, we hear Ryan playing his trumpet downstairs.

"Ryan, it's quarter to 6:00," I yell down to him. He finishes the last few notes of "Buttercup Baby" before coming up. Caitlyn left her clarinet at school, so the Whitten kids just have to worry about the correct belongings to bring.

When we get to the high school, the band already began warming up. We each take our proper seats with our sections. The woody taste of my reed sticks to my tongue. I place it in my mouthpiece, and I'm ready to go. "Crazy Train" is the next song Mrs. P. calls out. That's the last song of our warmup set before we go out.

In the gym the athletes are making layups. We start off playing our school song to get the crowd going.

At tip off, our team, the Tigers get the ball. The point guard makes a pass and we score a three pointer. I always believe whoever makes the first shot will win the game. I cheer loudly for our team. Tess sits in the bleachers nearby.

"Sweet Caroline!" Mrs. P. shouts. Each section passes the message on to the section behind them. She waits for everyone to hear it before she starts conducting.

 I push my three left fingers down to play a G. With each note I effortlessly push down the appropriate buttons. My instrument sings through the first verse and goes into the refrain. I feel my palms hurt. I squeak out a high-pitched note. Mrs. P. looks at me. In fear of messing up again I fake play the rest of the game.

As per tradition after pep band we go to Dairy Queen. I order a chocolate cone with cherry dip. The red color dip breaks off with each bite. The cold treat tingles against my teeth. Caitlyn and Ryan decide to share a banana split. Tess just gets a cup for water. We grab a booth by the window. Orange headlights beam through the glass.

"So, Jenna, you have an appointment it looks like tomorrow," Tess says, looking down at her calendar on her phone. I didn't expect for her to have my schedule accounted for yet. She continues, "It's with

Dr. Cooper, is that right?" She takes a sip from her DQ cup.

"Yep. Are you coming with?" I feel like that's a stupid question to ask but she confirms that she is. We wrap up our ice cream social and head home.

Mom and Dad are already back home by the time we get there. Tess is officially off the clock and leaves. I'm exhausted so I hit the hay. Caitlyn and Ryan stay up in the downstairs living space. Their laughter puts me to sleep.

14.

A shooting pain explodes through my legs. It wakes me from my slumber. The pain is so intense my legs stretch out straight. I hit the footboard with my toes. The cold metal doesn't help.

"Caitlyn! Wake up." I say through clenched teeth. I pull my knees to my stomach. The movement makes things worse. I throw a pillow at her. "Get mom. Now!" Without question she sprints upstairs. I hear her shouting Gail and Bill up the stairs. I close my eyes shut. I get a headache from it all. *Please God, please make this stop.*

"What's going on?" Mom asks in a panic. I can't respond. I just grab hold of my legs that are now tingling.

"We need to go to the hospital." Dad states. He gathers me up in his arms wedding style. Mom opens up the back seat of our black truck and dad sets me inside. Caitlyn stays behind. Dad climbs into the driver's seat and takes off.

The ride is bumpy due to all the potholes. *Damn you city streets.* Dad speeds through town to the hospital. When we get there, they grab a wheelchair for me to sit in. They rush me inside. Mom talks to the nurse at the front desk.

"Our daughter is having pain in her legs." She says in a single breath. "She has ALS." The lady looks down at me. Squinting in pain I make eye contact with her. They bring me back to a room that looks very sterile. Dad picks me up and places me in the bed. Soon a doctor who I haven't met comes in.

"Your daughter will be fine. We are going to give her an IV of potassium since her levels are low and her pain should subside." He then sticks a needle in the hinge of my left arm. Sure enough, the pain fades. I feel it leave just as quickly as it came.

"I suggest getting her a heating blanket. That will keep her muscles relaxed at night." My parents still look worried.

"What does this mean for her ability to walk?" Mom chokes out the words. A tear falls from her eye.

"You can discuss that with Dr. Cooper later today. It looks like you already have an appointment set up." I didn't realize it was this late. The white round clock reads close to 3:15. We leave for home once the IV is finished giving me the potassium.

The next morning Tess comes before I wake up. Mom and dad already left but I am sure they wish they could still be sleeping. I hear a light knocking on my door. *Screw this.* I roll over. Tess peeks her head in.

"Hey... um... it's time to get up," she informs me softly. She goes over to my closet and picks out comfy clothes, ones that are easy to slip on. I take notice in how my legs are now feeling. Although there isn't any pain, they feel absolutely exhausted. I'm afraid they won't be able to support my body weight.

"Last night was quite the event." I tell Tess as she pulls a sweatshirt over my head. A worried look takes over her face. I tell her about the pain and going to the ER.

'How are you feeling now?" She asks. I shrug.

"Exhausted." She seems to understand. She slips a pair of sweatpants on me. The comfy clothes make me feel content. Mom and dad bought me a walker last week just to be prepared. I'm now grateful that they did. Tess pulls out the red walker from the furnace room that's next to my room. She helps me up the stairs. With one hand on the railing and my other arm wrapped around her for support we make the climb. After seating me in a chair, she goes back down to retrieve the aluminum walker. It's just Tess and me in the car. Caitlyn rides with Ryan to school.

At school the embarrassment over takes my exhaustion. Through the hallways my walker leads my path. Students part ways like the red sea.

We walk into the student services office to talk to Mr. Porter about implementing my new schedule. Tess carries my bookbag to the next class.

Chemistry arrives and I am curious how Charlie will react. He's wearing a blue short sleeved shirt, revealing his Ninja Turtle tattoo on his bicep.

"Nice wheels you got there Jenna." He always makes me smile.

"Better than your beat-up heap of metal." I tease about his truck. Today we must take notes on balancing molecular formulas. I feel anxious about writing. I can't seem to trust my own body anymore. I look at Tess for reassurance. She stands up from her chair and takes a seat next to me in the empty desk.

"Maybe you can ask Mr. Vaughn if you can just print out the notes." She suggests. I take her up on the idea. Mr. Vaughn allows me to. I feel like such a slacker. Charlie's presence is at least nice. I get a text from mom. It reads that my appointment has been moved up to 10:00. That's during math, my next class. *Thank you, God.* I can't stand Geometry.

Mom picks me up at the front of school. I get in the front seat while Tess collapses the walker and puts it in the trunk. At the appointment, Dr. Cooper introduces himself to Tess.

"I am glad to see you have a caretaker." He compliments. I take a seat on the raised bed. He pinches my calves and flexes my feet. I am so use to the discomfort that I don't really react emotionally. He then examines my hands that lay limp in my lap. I can be compared to a rag doll that has just been propped up, wanting to come alive.

"How has your other therapy been going?" Dr. Cooper asks. I haven't seen Lynelle in a while now. We have been going to see her only when needed and with this new event I am guessing we will be seeing her very shortly.

"Give her a call." Doc tells mom. "With this new restriction we want to make sure her mind is stable." In the car mom calls Pricedecer Therapy Services. On the Bluetooth system the car's speakers explain we will have a session in two days at noon. I guess I'm looking forward to it.

15.

Tess takes me to my therapy appointment. She
waits in the lobby area while I have my appointment.
I step into Lynelle's office. She is already seated in
her rocker. I roll my walker and sit in the chair
instead of the couch. I'm afraid it's going to be too
hard to get up once I sit down. She seems to take a
mental note of this.

"Hi it's good to see you. Is there anything you would
like to talk about right away?" She asks. I feel like
I'm a kid in middle school being tested with a trick
question. I shake my head no.

"Alright that's fine." She continues. "I think talking
about grief will be a good start since you are
ultimately grieving the loss of your mobility." I never
thought of it that way before. I never thought I was
able to grieve for myself.

She brings out a few books. She explains that one
was written by a person who had multiple sclerosis.
Another book was a children's book about the
simple ability to say goodbye to lost things.

"I think both of these will help you to not feel alone in
all of this." She smiles. A sudden burst of anger fills
me. *A damn children's book doesn't comfort me.* My
furrowed brow gives her a clue to my frustration.

"Jenna, I know these books aren't exactly like your situation, but I still think they may help?" My strong emotion softens. She's a good counselor. She seems to know what to say in the right moment.

"I'll give them a try." My response makes her smile. She starts with the children's book to get it out of the way. We flip through the pages of cartoonish drawings saying goodbye to different things and people.

"So maybe as this disease takes over your body," Lynelle starts slowly, pausing before she continues, "you can say goodbye to each thing it takes." I choke back tears. *I'm supposed to say goodbye to my life? Just like that?* "I know this takes time Jenna. No one expects you to take this easily. You have people with you through this." And with that our session was over.

Tess drives us back to school. I'm just in time for English. I don't feel like going into the library for this class like I am supposed to. Mr. Porter moved it down there so I wouldn't have to go upstairs but I want some sort of normalcy.

We enter the elevator and illuminate the two button. Mrs. Stark seems to be surprised with my entrance. She clears a spot for me at her back work-table.

"Nice to have you in class." she says and gives me a wink. Caitlyn joins me. She asks how the appointment went with Lynelle. I shrug. I digress.

"How's your paper going?" She is comparing joy to food. If she could she would compare it to weed. She reads what she has already.

"A nice rich bite of chocolate, a juicy burger, creamy pasta." *You sound like you have the munchies.* Maybe she wrote this while she was high. "All giving a sense of pure joy. What do you think?"

"Sounds great." I lie. I get out my English notebook. I title my paper *A Sea of Sadness*. I write down *I look down into this glass of water. My image drowning in this depth of H20.* After this short beginning my hand can't take anymore. My start is not legible. I do my exercises Ashley suggested and I lay my pencil down. Tess saves me.

"Want me to write for you?" She proposes. I am grateful for this offer. She asks what my topic is.

"I am relating a concrete object, water with something abstract that being hopelessness." It sounds even more depressing out loud. She doesn't seem to be phased by it. She just waits for me to tell her what to write. "This clear liquid is suffocating. It's infinite. It's overwhelming." Blue ink scribbles down my dialect.

"Dude, you're killing my spirits." Caitlyn says. I ignore her comment. I want to portray how I'm feeling through this essay.

"Water has been seen as life, but this vast substance leaves me questioning hope." The school bell ends my prelude to this dismal essay.

Today Charlie is coming over after school. I meet him in the commons. He already has a cap covering his brown sinuous hair. We take his truck through the car wash before heading home. I lean against the concrete wall while he sprays it with water. He intentionally showers me as well.

"Knock it off you asshole." I joke. He claims it was an accident. "Let me wash it then." I just want to get him misted as well. He hands me the sprayer and prepares for what's to come. Turning his back to me I drench his shirt. He takes it off before we drive away. His skinny physique is attractive to me.

I reach over and touch his tattoo. I trace it lightly with the tip of my finger. He only has the outline done. He has to save money to get it colored in.

"Can I fill it in with Crayola markers?" I ask, slightly joking. He jolts his arm away.

"No way." He says, being protective of his tattoo. I laugh at his response. We pull into the driveway and he puts his damp shirt back on.

The house is empty. Mom and dad are still at work and I'm guessing Ryan and Caitlyn are hanging out somewhere. We head downstairs. The main floor has too nice of furniture and it's not as homey. Downstairs has the furniture we had before we remodeled. It feels more relaxing.

"What do you want to do?" Charlie asks. I want to do something that doesn't involve using my hands. So, pool and ping pong are out.

"Want to play a game." I suggest. *That seems safe enough.* I get out a deck of cards.

"We're playing strip poker?" Charlie asks, grinning widely.

"You wish." We decide to play cribbage. I deal out six cards to each of us. I peg four points and my hand holds a double run, so I move eight more. He moves a lousy two points from having a pair.

"Let's at least make this a little interesting. If I win..." He pauses to think, "You have to kiss me."

"And if, or should I say when you lose, you have to you have to give *me* a strip tease." As we move down the board it's a close game. We are both five points away from the winning spot. That means it's up to pegging. I keep an ace, a two, a three, and a five. I lay down my three. He makes it turn into a a twelve by using a nine. I lay down my two. He pegs two more points by getting it to 15. *Crap.* At the end I peg two points while he pegs another point. He counts first.

"15 two, a run of three so that's five." He wins. "Pucker up babe." He's such a stinker. The last time I kissed someone was at a party and we played truth or dare. The guy I kissed used too much tongue and he had bad breath.

Charlie puts a soft hand on my face and leans in. I close my eyes as we move in closer. His lips are soft. They move with passion. Our tongues freely tangle. I place my hand on his chest. I feel his heart beating fast. I break free from his lips and gently kiss his neck. He seems to relax. I move my body on top of his. He is now under me laying on the floor. I feel his boner hit my jeans. He puts his hand on my breasts and squeezes softly. I go back to kissing his lips. We sit back up. We finally unlock lips. It's the first time in a long time where I felt like I had some control.

"Good game." He says quietly. His phone goes off.

16.

I tell Caitlyn all about my time with Charlie when she and Ryan get home. She clings to every word I say.

"So, do you think you guys will date again?" She asks, all excited. I want to. I'm attracted to him and our personalities just work.

"We didn't get to talk about it really. He got called into work." I explain. I want to wait and see how we are on Monday before I get my hopes up. If it's awkward we'll just act like it never happened. "I hope we do. I haven't had a boyfriend in a while." We giggle over this possibility.

"Speaking of dating, I have to tell you something." I am already excited for her. "Ryan and I are together.'

"It's about time!" I exclaim. They have been close for years. "Oh my gosh!" I just realized something. "We could double date!" She claps eagerly at this idea. *We are such girls.* I want her to tell me all about it. She says they started dating after my incident at the hospital. And they had their first kiss at the playground of our junior high under the monkey bars.

Ryan comes down the stairs. "Did you tell her?" He asks and places his hand on the small of Caitlyn's back. I give them each a hug. I am so happy for them.

I ask Ryan to give me a ride to my physical therapy appointment. Tess felt sick so she left early. All three of us ride to my appointment. They drop me off and go spend some time alone.

"Use a rubber," I call to them as they pull away. Caitlyn sticks her hand out of the sun roof and flips me off. I laugh and head in for my appointment. Ashley has a roll of tape in her hands. She cuts off a long piece of it and marks a line on the carpet.

"Today we are going to work on balancing.' she states. My confidence suddenly leaves me. I have been using the walker for some time now. She senses my uncertainty.

"I'll help you," she assures. My toes line up with the end of the tape. I take a deep breath in. *You're on a goddamn tightrope Jenna.* I take my first step. The muscle that runs from my big toe to my heel cramps. I put my arms out. Ashley is behind me and spots me. I start tipping to the left. I fall off the line.

"That was great," she encourages. Now she has me stand on my tip toes and stretch up to the sky. I go up and down about ten times before I stand back on the line. This time I make it five paces. That's improvement. She tells me to try this at home.

That night I make a line in my bedroom. I remember when I had the balance and the strength to do a handstand. Now I can't even take more than five steps on a pretend balance beam. Frustration overcomes me. I tear the tape off and crumple it up. I throw the sticky ball in the trash.

Monday arrives and I wake up nervous for chemistry. Tess pulls out a comfy set of clothes, but I tell her I want to dress nicely. She puts me in a floral pattern skirt with a white top. I would usually be able to put my hair in a French braid easily, but my dexterity has faltered. Tess assists me in the task.

"Well don't you look nice." Caitlyn tells me in band. I appreciate her compliment. I just hope Charlie will think the same. I play my pep band music with a little more pep.

Chemistry finally arrives. I take my seat and ask Tess to put my walker behind a lab bench. I want to be seen as a pretty girl. Not a pretty girl with aluminum baggage. Charlie walks in and I can tell he dressed up a little too. He's wearing a dark blue button up tucked into jeans. I immediately feel turned on. Any guy who wears a nice shirt tucked in to jeans does it for me.

"Hey." My voice comes out slow and low. I clear my throat. "You look nice." My voice isn't any better. I take a sip from my water bottle. My throat doesn't feel scratchy. It feels like how you talk when you're in a middle of a yawn. Just an octave lower and without expanding the jaw.

"Thanks." He says with a slight tone of question. He brushes it off. "I want to take you on an actual date." My nerves settle. He likes me back. I place my hand over his on the desk.

"That would be lovely." Now he's relaxed. He plans to pick me up at 8:00 the next night. I want to know where we are going and what we're doing but he says it's a surprise. My excitement makes each class goes by fast. At lunch I tell Caitlyn the good news.

"See I knew you didn't have anything to worry about." She exclaims. But I do have something to worry about. All day my voice has gone from normal to a weird slow-motion type of tone. I knew this disease could affect my mobility but my voice?

Tess speaks up after seeing how cuddly Caitlyn and Ryan are being. "So, both of the Whitten kids have a significant other?" Ryan and I both shake our heads in pride to this question.

The next night Caitlyn and Tess help me get ready for my date. For the outfit I choose some leggings and purple cardigan. Once Tess gets me dressed, I sit in the small wooden chair that is placed in front of my mirror. Caitlyn goes to work on my makeup. She gives me a very natural look with limited eye liner and blush.

"I'm thinking just have my hair down. What do you think?" My friends' opinions have suddenly never been more important to me. They give their approval. I bring my clutch purse just in case and I'm all set to go.

Charlie arrives five minutes early. He's wearing the same jeans with a red flannel tucked in. He shakes hands with my dad. So far, he's making a very good impression.

"Mrs. Whitten, long time no see." He gives my mom a hug. She always liked Charlie, thought he was the best boyfriend I've ever had. I agreed with her.

"Ready to go?" I take his hand that he has out. I want to know what we're doing, where we're going. We are just about to leave but mom calls after me.

"Jenna, your walker." I can feel my cheeks getting red. *I left that stupid thing behind for a reason.*

"No worries Mrs. Whitten." Charlie scoops me up in his arms. I shriek in fun. He places me in the passenger seat. He backs out of the driveway and turns on the radio. A Billy Joel song plays through the speakers. Charlie grabs hold on my hand while the other steers the vehicle. I still have no idea where he's taking us. He makes a left and heads for the bookstore. I am so confused. He opens my door and picks me back up in his arms. I hang on tight around his neck. It's icy out and I'm afraid he'll fall.

He pushes open the front door to the shop. *Oh my gosh.* In the open area in front of the cash register he has built a fort out of books and blankets.

Four tall stacks of books hold up a blanket used to make a roof. He has lights stringed up above it. I wonder when he did this. He must have asked my dad if he could come in and set this up. Inside the fort there is a mini table with a beanie bag on either end.

"Shall we?" He asks as he sets me down. I take a seat in the purple bean bag set on the floor. It conforms to my body. On the small table there are two paper plates. As I wait for Charlie to join me, I take in the beautiful atmosphere.

There are battery lit candles around the circumference of the fort. The spines of the books are pointed inward. The two stacks by the entrance of the fort are fiction and nonfiction. And the other two are fantasy and romance. Each stack has a few of my favorite books. *Paper towns, Go ask Alice,* and, *A Walk to Remember* are just a few that catch my eye.

Charlie comes in with his arms full of stuff. He sets a pizza down from Pizza Hut and a liter of Coke. *How romantic.* But I wouldn't expect anything else from him. He flips open the cardboard box the pizza is set in.

"I believe your favorite." He says hopefully. Mushrooms and cheese, he got it right. We each grab a slice and start nibbling on it.

"What do you want to do after high school?" I ask him just to get a conversation started. He puts up a "wait a second" finger as he finishes the food in his mouth.

"I want to be a car mechanic." I should have guessed. He's very intrigued with cars and how they work. He says he plans on going to our local technical college to get his gen eds and then transfer to one of the state universities. He returns the question.

"Well I guess with everything that's been happening I don't know what I want to do." This realization saddens me. My future now looks pretty dismal. I feel my body rest heavily into the bean bag chair. I can feel it want to swallow me.

"No. Jenna, I want to hear your plan. I know you've had one before all of this, so I want to hear it." His response sparks some confidence in me. *He's right. I can do whatever I damn well please.* Now smiling I tell him my goals and aspirations.

"I want to go to Antioch University Midwest for teaching." He seems totally engaged.

"And what do you want to teach?" He asks. I put my slice of pizza down and wipe the grease off my fingers. I tell him English for junior high kids. He pours more soda into each of our glasses.

"That would be awesome. I can see it now." He raises his hands in front of himself. "Ms. Whitten English teacher." I nod my head in excitement. I can actually see it too. I have put all my plans on the back burner but now I bring them back into full view. I can totally still teach.

Once three fourths of the pizza are gone, he puts the box on the countertop by the cash register. He tells me I can take it home for leftovers.

"You know what we should have?" I ask him as he is outside of the fort. "A cold pizza place. Where they serve you cold pizza." I would buy from there all the time. He comes back in and confirms that would be a cool idea.

"Ready for the second part of our date?" I didn't realize there was more. I expected to be dropped off at home after this. It's 9:00 when we leave the store.

He drives us past the paper mill. He turns onto a back road that I'm not familiar with. It's now dark out. He has his brights on. Taking it slow on the turns of the road. We see a family of deer cross. Charlie pulls up to an abandoned house with a wide turn around. He has the car parked so the headlights are facing this flat side of the house.

"Hang on," he says before getting out of the car. Charlie goes to the back seat and pulls something out. He waves his hand to get my attention. I open my door to hear what he has to say.

"Can you turn my brights off please?" I pull back the lever to do so. He puts this box like device on the hood of the car. Charlie presses a button on top of it. On the side of the house is a projection of two animated dogs eating a bowl of spaghetti. Charlie gets back into the car.

"See you're the lady and I'm the tramp." He states. I laugh at this comment. He pulls a blanket from the back seat. His truck has a bench seat in the front. He scoots closer to me while draping the blanket over both of us. I snuggle up next to him, putting my legs under my butt. His body heat is radiating off of him. I close my eyes and just take in his warmth. My hand that is lying on his chest can feel his heartbeat. It's steady.

The movie is short and sweet. As the credits go through, I look up at him. He smiles before leaning in to kiss me. It's soft and light. He puts his hand into my hair. He finishes by kissing me on the forehead.

"Before I bring you home, I want to say something." He says. I look into his emerald eyes. They look serious. "I am in for the long run with this." He's talking about my disease. "But with that aside I am dating you for you. I want you. As you are." I feel myself getting emotional. I don't have a proper response for that, so I kiss him again. That was the perfect ending to a perfect night. He drops me off at home and I fall asleep with a smile on my face.

17.

Tess wakes me up from my happy slumber. Today I have to wash my hair. I wonder how this will work out. Tess brings my clothes to the bathroom. She picked out leggings and a long sleeve shirt. It's comfy and allows for easy mobility. She pulls off my night wear. I stand there naked shivering.

Mom and dad got this shower chair. I must climb over the edge of the bathtub to get to it. I hold onto Tess for stability. She rolls up her sleeves before turning the shower on. I sit with my back to the shower head so it doesn't spray my face. The water is cold at first. I quiver from the first mist.

The warm water kicks in and I relax. I grab the shampoo from its place. I squirt out a quarter sized amount into my hand. I bring it up to my now wet hair. After about ten seconds my arms get exhausted from lifting them. I place them in my lap. The water suds up the substance and drips down my body. I look to Tess for some help.

"Are you okay if I come in there with you?" I hesitate to respond because I know this will max out my ability to be embarrassed, but I don't know how else I'll wash my hair. She unbuttons her plaid shirt. I look away as she removes her bra. Once she is fully undressed, she steps in front of me. She spits out some more shampoo to really get my hair clean. Her fingers move in circular motions from the front of my scalp to the back. I can tell she is trying to hurry. I keep my eyes on her feet.

"Tilt your head back so it can rinse out well." *Dammit.* I try to look up quickly so I don't see anything, but I get a glimpse of her breasts. She gets closer to me as she runs her hands down the tail of my hair. *This is so uncomfortable.* I fold my arms across my shoulders to cover my own breasts.

"Almost done." She says. Tess takes a bar of soap and runs it down my body. I unfold my arms so she can get to my chest. She lets the soap run down my breasts and goes to my stomach.

"Can you try to turn around to face the water?" I swivel my body carefully in the chair. The steamy liquid rinses me off. Tess quickly gets dressed while I let the water wash over me. She turns off the shower and hands me a towel. I pat down my face and torso. She cloaks it over my shoulders and helps me get out of the tub. She takes the towel and pats down my legs. Tess hesitates as she gets closer to my upper thighs. The towel is damp by the time she finishes. Grabbing a new one she shakes my hair out.

With her help I get dressed. I've learned that closing my eyes eases the awkwardness. She then starts to blow dry my hair. The warm air relaxes me. It feels good hitting my ears and the back of my neck. She braids my hair into a side braid.

"Beautiful." Tess compliments her work once she's done. I notice it's quarter to 8:00 by the time we head upstairs. I grab a granola bar to go. I sit in her car while she folds up my walker and puts it in the back. I get a text from Charlie asking where I'm at. He was planning on meeting me before first hour. *Sorry, the task of showering took a bit longer than expected.* Tess backs out of the driveway and heads to school.

In band we are practicing for our next concert. A piece called "The Hexagon" is passed out. It switches from two-four-time signature and four-four time. I look forward to the rests so I can stretch my fingers out.

 I only squeaked twice during practice today. That's an improvement. I am finding that my body gives signals before fully freaking out. So my fingers might slightly twitch before cramping up on me. Charlie meets me outside of the band room.

"Hey you doing okay?" He greets. I reassure him that I am. We head to chemistry. Tess follows behind us. I move over so she can walk next to me. I don't want her to be a third wheel. Charlie places his hand on my back as we walk to the science wing.

Once getting to the classroom Mr. Vaughn has practice problem sets on the board. The grouping of desks Charlie and I sit at has to balance a formula. After each group is done one person has to stand up and share the answer. Charlie was a bit confused by it, so I volunteer to present. I can sense a bit of pride coming from Tess.

"I added three molecules to carbon," my speech dips in pitch when I say carbon. I clear my throat. "To balance out Florine." My voice is doing that weird thing again where it's speaking slower than it should. Standing up there with everyone's eyes peering between me and my walker I feel vulnerable. I sit down in my seat, keeping my eyes down. Charlie puts his hand over mine on the desk.

Math comes and for once I appreciate it. I don't know anyone in that class, so it spares me from talking. I sit down in my desk and do the ten problems were assigned. Today we are finding the angles within an inscribed circle. *I will never need this shit.* I finish the last problem just as the bell rings. I am happy the class went by fast. I'm looking forward for study hall because I get to see Charlie. He meets me outside of my math class. He seems upset.

"Hey. What's going on?" I touch his arm in hope he will soften up. He explains that a kid in his welding class messed up his project. He had been working on welding a lamp. Apparently, this other kid nudged Charlie's lamp off the table, causing it to break, while trying to grab his own project.

"Babe, I understand your frustration but I'm sure you'll figure it out." I comfort as I take his hand. He thanks me by squeezing my hand.

We walk over to study hall. In the hallway kids move towards the lockers to leave room for me and my walker. While passing by the water fountain, my right leg stays behind as my walker and my left foot moves forward. This causes my roller to glide ahead without me. I trip forward. My right leg feels numb while the other is aching in pain from hitting the ground. I tenderly grasp it.

"You okay?" Charlies asks while retrieving my walker.

"Yeah I guess." Tess helps me up. She and Charlie hold onto me on either side while I clutch tightly to my walker. Eventually we make it to Mrs. Stark's room. Once I'm situated in my desk Tess steps outside the room to call my mom.

Charlie inches his desk closer to mine. Worry is still seen in his face. I want to tell him that I'm okay, that everything is fine, but I don't even know myself if that's true. Tess comes back into the room and she seems to be a bit more relaxed.

"You have an appointment after lunch, Jenna." She confirms. I am happy to hear that. I am wanting to know what's going on with my voice. Charlie seems to be calmer about the matter. Now that there's a plan set in place, we use the study hall just to hang out.

Charlie pulls out a piece of paper and writes the word M.A.S.H. on the top in all caps.

"Ever play this game before?" He asks. I shake my head no. He explains M.A.S.H. stands for mansion, apartment, shack, and house. He then writes job, kids, car, and salary with choices under each category. This game looks intriguing.

"Now I'm gonna draw a zigzag line and you tell me when to stop." He draws about five connecting lines before I say stop. He counts the lines to confirm the number.

"Okay now I count to five and cross out the item I land on until there is one of each category. Get it?" He explains. This is like a fortune cookie type game. It tells you your imaginary future. He bends the piece of paper so I can't see the finale results.

"Drum roll please." He exclaims. Tess taps her fingers on the desk. "Ms. Whitten...your future…" He takes a deep breath in before revealing the results. "You live in an apartment with four kids. Your job is a Walmart greeter but somehow your salary is $400,000." My fake future isn't too bad. The easy-going game gives me a small sense of hope. Charlie seems to have met his goal with it. He has no idea how much I appreciate him.

18.

"Jenna, your voice is dipping in pitch, and as you described it talking in slow motion, because your vocal cords are also a muscle." Dr. Cooper explains. *You have got to be kidding me. Not my voice. Please God not my voice.* Everyone else in the room seemed to have known this. I figured it was due to ALS, but I guess I was naive enough to think it would leave me my voice.

"As for her legs. I see that you have a walker now, but have you thought about a wheelchair?" I was afraid of this as well.

"I don't want one." My shaky voice speaks up. I know I will have to eventually, but I am going to stretch out that time as long as I can. I will do whatever it takes to keep my mobility just a little bit longer.

"Okay but incidents like this has me concerned." Dr. Cooper responds. Mom says she agrees. I am seated in a chair next to his desk. In his spinny chair he rolls himself closer to me. He brings my foot up and takes off my shoe and sock. My big toe is curled inward from all the cramping. He tries to stretch it out so it lays straight. I wince from the pain. He lets go and it naturally goes back to that curled position.

"I am going to recommend you go to physical therapy twice a week then." Doc prescribes. "I see you have an appointment tomorrow. That's good." He takes a pause to show he's moving to a new topic of conversation. "How has it been going with Lynelle?" I haven't seen her in a while. Mom looks guilty as if she is at fault to this.

"We can schedule to see her every week." Mom says to save herself. Dr. Cooper thinks that's a good idea.

"We are trying to keep your body happy and we need to do the same for your brain." He says while taping his finger on my noggin. With having those appointments penciled in our calendar we leave.

Mom goes back to work, and Tess takes me home. Ryan skips up the steps from downstairs. He helps me while Tess brings my walker down to the basement.

"How'd that go sis?" He asks. In habit I clear my throat even though I know that won't help.

"Not great. Doc mentioned a wheelchair." I say in disappointment.

"Nah Sis screw that. I'll give you piggyback rides before that happens." I love Ryan. He understands that my pride is at risk every time this disease tries to take something away from me. Ryan picks me up just to show he isn't joking. He brings me downstairs and gently tosses me on the couch. Tess helps me sit up. I pull out a folded-up note that has my homework assignments scribbled down on it.

Today I just have English. We are now on the poetry unit. I got an A on my *Sea of Sadness* paper with some encouraging commentary from Mrs. Stark. Now we are doing "Just Because" poems. Tess takes a seat next to me on the couch. I hand her my notebook and pencil. She is now my scribe for any writing assignment.

"Just because poems?" Confusion hints her voice.

"Yeah like just because I'm a girl doesn't mean I like pink." I give as an example. She seems to have a bit more of an understanding. My mind goes blank on what I want to write about. I don't want to do anything cliché.

"Jenna, what about 'just because I have ALS…'" Tess suggests. That didn't even cross my mind. I ponder it for a second.

"Just because I have ALS…" Tess smiles at the fact that I took her suggestion. "Doesn't mean I am weak." I wait for her to write it down. Ryan sits pretzel legged on the floor. He acts as my audience for a poetry reading. "Doesn't mean I am incapable.

Doesn't mean I can't manage. I am strong." Tess writes down this stanza. Ryan is smiling brightly with pride for me. I can't help but smile myself. "Just because I have ALS doesn't mean I like pity. Doesn't mean I don't feel vulnerable. Doesn't mean people's looks don't affect me. I am human." I start to get emotional. I continue. I feel like I'm on a roll now. "Just because I have fucking..." I pause to swallow my tears. "ALS doesn't mean my spirits are dying. Doesn't mean I'm not happy. Doesn't mean I am fading away. I am still here." Tears are rolling down my cheeks. Tess hugs me while Ryan snaps in encouragement.

19.

Ashley pulls out this blue circular balancing tool. She directs me to take my shoes off.

"I want you to try to stand and balance on this." She says with complete faith that I can do it. The object has small grooves in it. I place my right foot on the right side of it and mount onto it with my left. The depressions feel good on my feet. I stay steady on it for about four seconds before my weight shifts and I fall off. I do this for about five more times, gaining a second more on each time before we move on to a different exercise.

"Do you have your stretch band?" Ashley asks, looking between me and Tess. It's in my backpack. Tess pulls it out and hands it over to me. Ashley has me stretch out each leg while she grabs something from her desk drawer. I put the band around my foot and pull back with the handle in my hand. My fingers flinch and the band flings forward. It comes close to hitting Ashley in the ankles.

"Nice aim." She says jokingly and hands it back to me. This time I put the handle near the joint of my elbow and pull back. This gripping works much better.

Ashley pulls out this bulky looking sock. "There are two tennis balls in here." She hands it to me. "I want you to put this under your feet and roll out your muscles." She points to my hand, "It's the same concept you do with a pencil for your hands." Tess offers to help me stand up.

I put one foot on this device and keep the other steady next to it. Tess stands close to me so I can use her shoulder for balance. I feel the tendons in my foot move in the side to side direction I'm moving the ball in. I switch to the other foot.

"It looks like your session is up, but I'll let you keep that one. I can easily make more." Ashley says to end our appointment.

The sun shines brightly into my eyes as I leave the dim lighted building. I shade my eyes and I see a white pickup truck with red rims. In the driver seat is a thin guy dressed in white t shirt. Charlie honks his horn.

"Can I steal her from you?" He yells from his window. Tess gives him her permission.

"If you need anything, I'm a phone call away." Tess tells me. She helps me make it over the icy parking lot to his truck before she leaves.

"You ready to go for a ride, Jenna?" He asks in a snarky tone. Before I can answer he guns it out of the parking lot. *Dear Lord, help us.* He drives over to highway 47. He makes a quick right turn onto a snowy backroad.

"Unbuckle." He says as he does the same. I question my safety, but I do it anyway. "Okay now keep your finger on the window control."

"Why?" I ask before doing so. I look over at him. He is smiling and staring forward. I turn my attention to what he's looking at. The car is parked just before a lake. He accelerates the car forward. He breaks and turns a knob on his dash. He switched to four-wheel drive.

"Now we're cooking with gas." He exclaims. I take a glance at the speedometer. We are going 40mph on this sheet of glass like ice. He swerves to the left. As a driver he's having more fun than me. I smile as I grab hold of the passenger handle. "Feeling unsafe there babe?" He asks with such tease in his voice. He pats my knee. I grab and squeeze his hand back to show I trust him. He does donuts. No one else is on the lake except us. It provides some sort of peace in the madness of his driving.

We head back once the sun starts to go down. I stare back in the rearview mirror and see the amber sun disappear into the horizon.

20.

I share my "Just Because" poem with Lynelle.

"Wow Jenna. That is really empowering." She
beams. "I want you to keep this and look at it
whenever you are feeling inadequate." I smile at the
idea of empowering myself. I've been looking to
other people to do that. Charlie, Ryan, Caitlyn, but I
can do that myself. "You seem to really enjoy
writing. Maybe we can use that in your therapy."

I like that idea. Maybe I can express myself
properly then. She gets a pad of paper and a pen
from her desk.

"So, if you have anything you want me to write go
ahead, otherwise I have a writing prompt for you." I
think of what I can say. Suddenly my mind is blank. I
look around the room for inspiration. In the left
corner of the room is a box of toys for her younger
clients. On a table behind her she has some hand
sized instruments like shakers and a tambourine. I
got nothing. "Want a prompt?" She asks after giving
me a few seconds to think.

"Yes please." I respond. Lynelle writes something
down on top of the page.

"Start with I remember and go from there." She
pauses to write something else down. Maybe the

date. "And every time you get stuck go back to that phrase 'I remember'" I pause to think about what I want to say.

"I remember…" I think of the right words to say. "I remember when I didn't have ALS." I pause for her to write this down, but I want to keep going. "I remember being able to run and walk. To be able to write my own name neatly. I remember having fun with friends when this stupid disease didn't get in the way."

My mind goes off on another tangent. "I remember when Charlie and I dated the first time we wrote down a bucket list." I try to recall what was on that bucket list. "We wanted to have a movie marathon of all Lord of the Rings movies. We wanted to go go-karting."

I move onto another memory with Charlie. "I remember the first time kissing him. We went to homecoming together but decided to leave early." I smile at this thought. We went for maybe an hour before we decided it was too boring. He brought us back to my place. We went downstairs and talked about the farthest we have each gone with another person. I was pretty innocent compared to him. "I remember we went into my bedroom. I told him I had never French kissed someone before." Lynelle is a fast writer. "I remember him leaning in and feeling his faint mustache hitting my upper lip."

When our tongues met, I didn't exactly know what to do so I let him guide me. "I remember him treating me with such respect. He would ask several times before doing anything." I stop and see that he is still, if not more respectful to me now. "I remember why we broke up. He felt like we were better off as friends. We only dated a short while." Maybe that's why he wanted to date again. We have been friends for over a year now so he knows we will work well together. With sharing that last thought our session was over.

Caitlyn comes over after the appointment. We go into my room and pull out my laptop. I know what that means. Pretend shopping on Amazon. We scan through many different items that look appealing and add them to our cart. At the end we scroll down and see everything we would have bought if we had the money. The price total always shocks us.

"I found a good one." I exclaim, bringing the image to a bigger size. It's a cute jacket with zippers on the sleeves. It costs $60. I add it to the cart. I pass the laptop over to Caitlyn. She picks out a pair of leggings and a stylish backpack. Our shopping cart is escalating in price. We step away from clothes and accessories and move on to interior design items.

"Hey, I found a cool coffee table." Caitlyn says, showing me her find. We have discussed moving in together once we graduate. Pretend buying for our future apartment is fun. I pick out a rug with a zigzag pattern across it. Our accent color is a turquoise blue. In the search bar at the top of the webpage I type in bedding. A bunch of different prints come up. I click on one that has a tie dye pattern of different shades of blue. It goes along perfectly with our imaginary setup. After adding about ten more items we look to see our total price. It's well over $1000. We exit out of the website and feel quite satisfied with ourselves.

"Wanna run over to the bookstore? I want to get a new read." I ask. Tess is upstairs getting dinner prepared. Mom is working late tonight. Once Tess is done peeling carrots we ask if she wants to join.

"Sure. I've never been there before." She replies while washing her hands. We hop into her car and drive to the shop. Tess parallel parks behind dad's truck. The window of the store has a decal that says "Whitten's Written Word." A ding of a bell signals we have entered the shop.

"Who's there?" Dad asks from behind a bookshelf. It's quarter to six so the shop is going to close soon.

"Just us." I respond. I head over to my favorite genre, nonfiction. I pick up a book titled *My Loving Wife in the Psych ward.*

"Hey. Whatcha guys doing here?" Ryan asks as he comes around the corner. I jump. I didn't know he was here. He laughs at my natural response. "Easy there, Spazz." I lightly slap his arm.

"We got bored and Jenna wanted a book." Caitlyn answers his original question. She gives Ryan a quick hug. I look back down at the book that is in my hand. I read the back cover.

When Giulia was twenty-seven, she suffered a terrifying and unexpected psychotic break that landed her in the psych ward for nearly a month. I'm sold. I go behind the cash register and pull out a clipboard. If any of us family members want to read a book, we check it out on the clipboard. It lets dad know what's missing from his inventory.

"Are you staying the night?" Ryan asks Caitlyn. She gives a thumbs up. Tess walks past me to the romance novels. She picks up a book by Nicholas Sparks. I didn't peg her for a romance reader. That made me realize I don't know that much about Tess. Is she married? Is her dad still alive? What's her favorite color?

"*Fifty Shades of Grey* should be back there somewhere." Ryan calls to her.

"Shut up." Caitlyn elbows him in the ribs. *Ryan you're such an asshole.*

"Already own it." Tess calls back. I catch her eye. She winks. I want to have some alone time with Tess. Not help me get changed alone time but go grab a coffee alone time. I want to get to know her. Maybe we can do something this weekend.

"Unless you kids want to help close up shop, I suggest you leave now." Dad says. We scurry out of there.

21.

Saturday afternoon is pretty relaxed. Caitlyn is helping her mom around the house, so it allows me to have some alone time with Tess that I have been craving.

"Have you ever had sushi?" I ask her. There is a sushi restaurant the next town over. It's about a half hour ride but it's so worth it.

"Nope. 28 years old and I've never had it." That's a sin in my book. I grab my wallet from the mudroom closet. "It's on my bucket list though."

"We're going." I say. She likes the idea of trying something new. I get into the passenger seat. I press the button to turn the seat heater on. The leather warms up my back. I pull my chair closer to the heating vents. The warmth makes me cozy. Tess backs out of the garage and we're on our way.

"Wanna play 50 questions?" I ask so I can get to know her.

"50's a lot don't you think? Let's do 15." I agree to her suggestion. I ask if she wants to come up with the questions or should I.

"Let's alternate." I think that's a good idea. I start. I ask her what her favorite color is.

"Purple." I should have guessed. Her wardrobe has a lot of purple in it and her purse is purple as well. I consider that to be a too girly of a color. Mine's red. It's her turn for a question.

"Favorite pet?" I say dog. We both agree on this. We get into a small conversation how my dad won't allow for any pets.

"We had a cat, but he died. 23 years old." Tess is shocked by this. "My dad hated that damn cat. But it came along with dating mom." She laughs at this statement. "Favorite movie?"

"Oh, that's a good one. Give me a second." She turns onto Highway K. The trees are outlined with snow. The banks are knee high. I feel bad for the deer who have to jump over it.

"Okay I got it. My favorite movie is..." She pauses to focus on her driving. There's a car pulled over with its emergency lights blinking. Tess drives around them. "That's Life!"

"What's it about?" I'm intrigued. I'm a movie fanatic but I've never heard of it. I guess its genre in my head.

"Well it's a drama." I guessed correctly. "I haven't seen it in gosh 20 years, but I remember just loving it."

"It's your favorite movie and you don't own it?" I'm perplexed. I own all my favorite movies.

"It's rare which makes it expensive." She says. There's a bit of silence as if we are mourning this loss. I break it by stating it's her turn to ask a question.

"Question number three. Here we go. What is your favorite childhood memory?" I like that she is taking it to a more personal level. I mull over this question. So many come to mind.

 The time when Caitlyn and I had a sleepover in the treehouse, and we played truth or dare? We ended up running around the treehouse naked. Or going up North for Christmas and sledding down the closed run at night with my cousins? When Ryan and I were kids we would have arcades set up in our rooms and charge quarters for each game.

"My favorite childhood memory is when I was in junior high, I was in band." I laugh at the recollection of this. "I was an overachiever and I got a 200% in the class. I would ask the band director what extra credit or other songs I could work on to gain a better percent for my grade." Bless that teacher's heart.

"She was so patient with me." Tess laughs at the idea of me being an annoying 13-year-old.

Tess shares her favorite childhood memory is learning how to knit and cross stitch with her mom before she died. I point to the light purple scarf around her neck.

"You made that?" She nods yes. I am impressed.

"These mittens too." She wiggles her fingers on the steering wheel. By the time we get to the town of Walden, we have gotten through 14 questions. I have learned that her lucky number is 21, she has never been pulled over, her dad is still alive, and that she her birthday is March 28th. It's her turn to ask the last question.

"How are you doing?" I think that a strange question. She elaborates as she sees I'm confused. "How are you doing with everything. With having ALS. How are you doing?" She's never asked me this before. I just assumed she thought I was fine, but I guess I haven't asked myself that question either.

"I am doing..." I really need to think. "Okay. Honestly, I'm scared." She turns down the heat that is blasting so she can hear me better. She doesn't say anything yet. She lets me continue. "I can handle it taking my legs and arms, not excited about it but I can handle it, but my voice? When Dr,

Cooper said I have three to five years I didn't really believe him but everything's happening so fast. What if it's sooner than that. I already feel weak." Tess parks in a parking lot across from the sushi place. She looks over at me, giving me full attention. "But the question I struggle with the most is why me?"

"Jenna, I understand your anguish with this. You must know how strong you are though too. Most kids are worried about finals and here you are battling this terrible disease. Kiddo, whatever this disease has thrown at you, you have taken it by the horns and dealt with it. I know you will continue to do so. And don't forget your wonderful support system, me included is there for you. You got this." I appreciate her sympathy. She gives me a quick awkward hug from her seat and we go off to enjoy our sushi.

"This stuff is really good." Tess says after trying a salmon roll.

"I told ya." We scratch it off her bucket list.

22.

It's Sunday and mom wakes me up for church. I haven't been in a while. I guess I've been kinda mad at God. This is Tess's day off in the week, so mom helps me get ready. She holds up a sundress with flowers on it. I turn it down. I don't want my legs to be cold as well as disabled. I want to put on leggings and a loose long sleeve shirt.

¨I´m just trying to make you feel better Jenna. If you look better, you'll feel better." I ignore her motherly advice and wait for her to scrunch up the pant legs of my leggings. When we get upstairs the boys are all ready to go. Dad doesn't change from his jeans and button-down shirt. Ryan has a straw hat on top of his head. Even though it's winter he still likes that summer vibe.

¨Is the gang all ready to go?" Dad asks, grabbing the car keys. We answer by exiting the mudroom to the truck. Ryan gives me a hand in climbing into the back seat. I sit there while he buckles me in. My hands won't allow for the dexterity to snap it into the buckle. We drive to the church. I am so familiar with the route. We drive through three stop lights and we're there. The church is connected to a Catholic school which I attended up to eighth grade.

At church our spot in the back has moved to the very front in the handicap area. I have learned that disability doesn't discriminate against age, gender, or ethnicity. It's a bitch in that way. My family sits a few rows behind me. They aren't allowed to take up space in this secluded area.

I take a spot next to Ruth, a 70-year-old grandma who just conformed to walking assistance herself. It feels weird not to genuflect before sitting in the row. To look like everyone else I bow my head in pretend prayer. *God, I don't know what to say to you. You kind of screwed me over.* Mass begins with the welcoming song "Jesus You Are Welcome Here." This is the first time I've felt happy about not being able to sing.

"Please stand, if you are able." Father's words seem to be targeted at me. I make my shaky legs stand. I do a death grip on my walker that is in front of me. The unstable stance empowers me because I fell like I proved Father Henry wrong. *Take that you condescending asshole.* He does a short opening prayer, asking for the Holy Spirit to be with us through this worshiping time.

The service goes by pretty fast. The sign of peace is now here. I turn to either side of me and shake hands with my neighbor. My family comes to hug me.

"You are strong. You are beautiful. You've got this." Mom whispers in my ear and she gives a strong embrace. I don't have a response for her, so I just hug with the same amount of strength. An acoustic song is strummed out while communion starts. Father comes to my section first.

"Body of Christ." The tall, overweight priest says to me. I open my mouth for him to place the tiny eucharist on my tongue. I don't trust my hands to not drop it. I break the crispy bread against the top of my mouth. I skip out on the blood of Christ.

The mass ends with an older gentleman up at the podium announcing there is a pancake breakfast in the school gym. We wait for everyone to make their way out before we exit our pew. Dad is talking to one of his friends who also owns a small shop.

Mom drapes my jacket over my shoulders. She walks along side of me as we head for the gym. Her body next to me makes a boundary between myself and anyone who might get in my way.

Ryan and dad take a spot in the short line while mom and I find a place to sit. She briskly walks to a table where the end chair is empty. It's perfect for me and my walker. We set our coats on the back of the neighboring chairs.

"Do you want regular or chocolate chip pancakes?" Mom asks.

"What do you think?" I grin brightly. She brings back chocolate chip ones. She takes a fork and knife and cuts up my food, as if I am five again. But I can't do it myself, so I have to deal with the embarrassment.

My thumbs are crumpled into the center of my palms with my fingers scrunched as well. Straightening them out will cause for discomfort so I let them be. I take the fork in my left hand and place it weaved between my index, middle and ring finger. I stab a slice of pancake and I lose the grip of the fork. It falls out of my fingers and splashes syrup at me. Mom scoots the plate back.

"Here." Mom dips her napkin into her water glass and dabs at the sticky splotches on my shirt. I reach for my fork to try again. Mom rests her hand over mine before I can get to it. She picks up the fork herself and feeds me the breakfast. *Keep it together, Jenna. I know you feel like a baby, but you'll be one even more if you cry.* Mom notices my red cheeks.

"Why don't we just take yours to go?" She suggests. I feel my overheated skin cool down.

The rest finish their plate. When we get home, I get a text from Caitlyn. *I see you just pulled in. Can I come over?* I tell her sure. Without even being able to put my food in the microwave she is at the front door. She enters through our mudroom. Caitlyn truly is part of the family. Before even saying hi to me she acknowledges Ryan.

"Good to see you too." I tease. She rolls her eyes.

"You know I love you too," is her response. They head downstairs while I reheat my breakfast. Mom grabs it from the microwave when it beeps. The plate is hot. I turn it with a napkin as a barrier between my hand and the steaming plate.

I use two hands on the fork now. With caution I bring the food up to my mouth. The first bite is so good. Mom leans against the counter, sipping her coffee, looking at me closely.

"Do you want help?" She offers. I shake my head no. I think it tastes so good because of the effort I'm putting into it. It takes me a solid twenty minutes to finish the two pancakes and glass of skim milk.

To get downstairs mom puts my arm around her neck. She guides me to the couch before she goes back upstairs to grab my walker.

"Do you need anything else?" She asks hopefully. I think she feels inadequate since Tess has really taken over the role of caring for me.

"A dog." Mom rolls her eyes. Ryan is terrified of them and dad doesn't want the extra responsibility.

Mom slugs back upstairs knowing I am okay for now.

Caitlyn and Ryan are snuggled up on this circular chair in front of the tv. They are watching an episode of *Friends*. Three male characters and three female characters are displayed on the flat screen. The show is popular enough, so people compare themselves to one of the characters. I think I am most like Rachel. She's smart, has a crush on her best guy friend, and likes fashion.

I get a text from Charlie. He's asking what my plans are for the night. This could be a perfect time to have a double date. I bring it up to the couple that's in the room.

"Yeah sounds great. Wanna go bowling?" Ryan suggests without thinking. "Oh I´m sorry Jenna. We can do something else." He corrects. I refuse to try another option. I haven't gone bowling in years. We schedule to go at 4:00 and to have pizza there. Charlie is also on board for the plan.

We meet Charlie at Lenny Lanes. I ask for a size ten shoes. Lenny hands me a lime green and orange pair of shoes. Ryan goes to our assigned lane and gets the game set up.

"Hey Jenna, what do you want your name to be?" I see he has his name as Bowlerpro, Caitlyn's is Cruising Cait, and Charlie's is just his name.

"How about Winner?" I say to top Ryan's name. He rolls his eyes and adds it in. Ryan is set up first to go. He knocks down four pins. On his second turn he hits down another five. He was so close to a spare.

Caitlyn doesn't do too well. She gets five pins down total. When it gets to my turn, I think of how I'm going to do this.

I ask Charlie to put the ball, the weight of it scored at a six, into my arms. I go up and set it just before the border. I rock it back and forth a few times before pushing it down the lane. It slowly rolls forward. It veers left and goes into the gutter.

"Excuse me?" Caitlyn calls to one of the employees. A man who seemed to be in his early 20s comes over. He looks annoyed that we bothered him from his day dreaming. "Can we have the bunkers put up?" The guy grabs a pole from behind the shoe rack. He jimmies the pole into the side of the lane and pulls up two walls. On my second turn I hit down three pins.

The game goes by pretty fast. Charlie scored two strikes and one spare. He is in the lead with 62 points. My ´winner´ title isn't comparing well with my low score of 36. Once we finish the game, we order a medium barbeque chicken pizza with a pitcher of Sprite. The slightly sweet taste of the barbeque sauce warms my mouth. The soda is fizzy down my throat.

"Wanna play another game?" Ryan asks. We decide not to. That we have had enough fun for one night. I nibble more on my slice of pizza. The doughy crust clumps in my back molars. I feel a cough coming on. I put my elbow up to my mouth. A bit food gets spit out into my sleeve. I try to catch my breath, but my chest is burning. Charlie hands me my glass of soda. It makes it worse. With eyes closed I try to set the plastic cup down. I miss the table and it falls to the ground. It splashes my jeans. My cough becomes worse. I gasp for air.

"Jenna, just breathe," guides Ryan. Charlie is on the other side, rubbing my back. It feels like there is a vacuum sucking the air out of my lungs. I start to panic. I bring a hand up to my throat to signify I need help. I make it clear that I need dire assistance.

"Should we call 911? Caitlyn frantically asks. I nod my head yes, wanting this wheezing to subside. "Hi yes. My friend can't breathe. We are at the bowling alley." There's a pause. I hear the other end mutter the question if I am choking. I shake my head no.

Caitlyn passes on the message. "None of us know CPR." She tells the operator. Caitlyn hangs up the phone and tells me they are on their way. My breathing is quick and short. *The hospital isn't too far away.* I tell myself repeatedly. Within the next five minutes the medics are here.

"Call her parents." A young nurse commands my small group of friends. Ryan steps aside and dials mom. Dad went to the bookstore to do some last-minute work before the week starts. Another medic guides me onto a stretcher. I sit up on this rubber padded seat. They bring an oxygen mask up to my face. It covers my mouth and nose.

"That's it... slow long breaths." The blonde medic guides. They bring the stretcher into the back of an ambulance. None of my friends can join.

The ambulance drives the short way to the hospital. By the time I get there my breathing is back to normal. I feel sweaty from all the panic I was in. I am loaded off the ambulance and brought to a small room with another bed inside. I am transferred to it and wait for the doctor to come in. A nurse brings mom back to the room.

"Are you okay? What happened?" Mom asks quickly. I shrug my shoulders. I'm not sure what exactly happened. They switched me from the bigger oxygen mask to a nose tube. The plugs in my nostrils tickle. Dr. Cooper knocks on the door frame.

"Is it okay to come in?" He asks before entering. He has my file with him. It's thick with lots of papers shoved into it. His face looks very certain about something. I'm afraid of what he has to say.

 "I bet today was scary for you." He starts. Mom vigorously nods. "I think it's time to make some changes for the better Jenna." I fearfully know what he means by that. "I think it's time to get you into a wheelchair. Your body wasn't taking in oxygen because it was over worked."

Okay so I won't go bowling again but that doesn't mean I can't walk. I keep the protest to myself. Doc explains that my legs are taking on too much stress from walking and my lungs are also a muscle, so the disease will eventually take over them completely.

"What does that mean for the future though. Dr. Cooper?" Mom asks with worry.

"Like I told you Gail this is a progressive disease." I can tell he wants to remind us of my life span, but he holds off. We leave after he gives us an oxygen tank to take home to be used at night. I get wheeled out in a wheelchair. I sit there in disappointment in myself.

23.

At school even more heads turn in my direction. I no longer have any classes upstairs, that includes English. I at least still get to have chemistry with Charlie. But band is out of the question. Mr. Porter schedules a meeting with my parents and myself to discuss graduation again.

"Mr. Whitten are we worried about graduation at this point or is the focus just elsewhere?" Mr. Porter begins the meeting. Dad seems to be offended. But that is a valid question for a guidance counselor to ask.

"Right now, we are worried about other things than graduation." Dad says in a fixed tone. They discuss what classes should be placed in the open slots, the ones I physically can't participate in.

"Well I was thinking since she can't do band and that is the first hour of the day, she can come in at second hour instead." Mom suggests. I at least get to sleep in with that idea. I´m on board for it. Mr. Porter agrees to this. Our meeting ends just before my chemistry class starts.

Tess rolls me into Mr. Vaughn's class. He sets me up at the back table that he has cleared off. Charlie moves his stuff to sit by me. I thank him by squeezing his hand. He hangs on to my hand a bit longer. He doesn't seem like he wants to let go. I let it be.

¨Are you doing anything after school?" Charlie asks in hope. I tell him I have an appointment with Lynelle. He seems to be disappointed. I wonder what he had planned. "I just wanted to spend more time with you is all." *You're so sweet.*

¨Well if you want to stop by after, say 5:00 that'll work." I cheer him up. Mr. Vaughn hands out the test and we become quiet. I place the test between Tess and myself and point to the letter answer I want her to circle. That class with the rest of the day goes by fast.

Mom joins me in the session with Lynelle. Tess went home since mom was able to take over. I feel like mom might get more out of this session than I will. Lynelle is wearing a green sweater dress pulled over brown leggings. We all take our usual spots.

"Symptom accommodation." She says to the both of us. Neither of us knows what that means. She has it written on her yellow pad of paper. A short paragraph is written underneath it to explain what it is. - *are the actions taken by parents, siblings, family members, friends, teachers and anyone who unintentionally reinforces a behavior.* "Gail for you as a parent this is really important. I will give an example to help you understand." She pauses to come up with one. "Say Jenna becomes depressed and she doesn't want to go to school. If you were to into that wish that would be accommodating her symptoms of depression, which would be a lack of interest in things. Makes sense? Now with her physical restrictions cutting back on chores like shoveling the walk way at home, obviously she physically can't do that so that is not symptom accommodation. Get it?" Mom nodes her head. She puts her hand out to get the notepad from Lynelle. She looks down at it to reread what is written. Her glasses slip further down her nose.

"What about allowing her to sleep in through the first period since she doesn't have a class?" It's a good question mom asks. I am hoping that won´t be an issue. I´m just so tired in the morning.

"Well is she not going because she physically needs the rest or is she just not wanting to go to school?" This is a rhetorical question. "See? So, no, that wouldn't be symptom accommodation cause her body has been working all day and is exhausted."

The session ends with another set-in place for tomorrow. We are having two sessions a week now and that's the only other day we could get in. Mom and I both learned something this session so that's good. I'm just happy I don't have to get up tomorrow morning. It's only quarter to five and I'm exhausted.

"I'm going snowshoeing." Mom says when we get home. "Will you be alright here by yourself?"

"Yeah Charlie will be here soon anyway." I reassure her. I´m in my room when Charlie gets here. He skips down the steps before I can even roll myself out of my doorway.

"Hey babe, how's it going?" He asks and leans down to kiss me. I smile when we unlock lips. He has on his usual green sweatshirt. I pull him in close for a hug and inhale deeply. He smells like the outdoors and campfire smoke. He goes behind to push my wheelchair out to the living space.

My feet lay barefoot on the foot rests of the wheelchair. The metal is cold against my heels. When the chair is positioned next to the couch, I grab hold of his arms to set myself onto the couch.

"Yes! My turn!" Charlie says as he gets into my wheelchair. He spins the wheels as he makes his way around the pool table. I shake my head in his delight. "Jenna check this out." I look over to see him doing a wheelie.

"Babe you are gonna actually get hurt and wind up in one for real. Knock it off." I can't help but laugh at his silliness. He sets himself back on all four wheels.

"You always take such good care of me." He says before kissing me on the couch. Charlie scoots me over so I am laying the long way on the couch. He gets on top of me, pressing his tongue further in my mouth. My arms are squished between our bodies.

"Babe, hang on." He backs off. I move my arms out of the way. He takes this opportunity to take his shirt off. He hairy stomach and chest stand out to me. I bring my hands up to the back of his head and we continue our lust for each other. He places his hand on my left breast and squeezes softly. My fingers tangle in his thick hair.

Charlie moves to kissing my neck. I feel his lips suction the tendons. *I am definitely going to get a hickey.* But I don't care. I feel myself getting warm from his weight on top of me. He scoots his body down so his face is at my stomach. His hands are under my shirt, unhooking my blue bra. He throws it on the coffee table next to us. He's gonna have to help me get it back on. Charlie kisses my stomach. I place my hand under his chin and have him meet my eyes. "Let's not go too far, babe." My words are breathy from being turned on. He brings himself back to my eye level.

"It's your call, but I agree." He smiles before giving me one last soft kiss. His shirt is pulled over his thin body. A hand is offered to help me sit up right. He helps me get my bra back on. It takes him a few tries before he hooks it correctly.

"Bet you never thought you'd do that before." I comment. We laugh at the reality we both find ourselves in.

"Kiddo, I'm home." I hear mom call from upstairs. *Perfect timing.* Charlie carries me upstairs. He's strong. It makes me feel protected. Mom's cheeks are red.

"Cold out there?" I ask. She nods and rubs her hands together to cause friction.

"Windy," she confirms. I look out of the kitchen windows that are over the sink. Gusts of wind pick up snow and flutters it through the air. Charlie sits me in my chair at the dining room table. He offers to help mom make dinner. She lets him chop vegetables for the chicken dumpling soup.

It's a good half hour before dinner is ready. Ryan is at Caitlyn's house tonight to celebrate their two-month anniversary. It feels weird without them here. Dad pulls into the driveway just as we are serving ourselves the delicious soup.

Mom takes the other seat next to me. Charlie is on my right and she is on my left. I try to feed myself but give up once the broth spills down the front of my shirt. Mom then takes over. She slices the dumplings into smaller pieces with the side of the spoon. The mushy dumplings cake onto my teeth. I use my tongue to slide the food to the back of my throat.

After dinner my dad gives a sturdy handshake to Charlie to signal it's time for him to leave. He leans down to give a goodbye kiss before he heads out.

"Drive safe." I call after him as he shuts our front door behind him.

24.

Dr. Copper hits my knee with a triangular hammer. There is no reflex. My knee just sits there tingling.

"I don't think continuing to see Ashley would be beneficial any longer." He states. Dad makes it visibly clear that he understands. I am conflicted. I hate physical therapy, but I love having that extra support.

"What about my hands?" I ask and show they still barely work by raising my arms and wiggling my fingers. Dr. Cooper validates my feelings.

"I know you like seeing Ashley and I am sure if you ever need her, she will be right there." He says in reassurance. The only person I wish I didn't have to see anymore is Dr. Cooper but that isn't going to ever happen.

The appointment was in the morning so dad brings me to school once it's done. Tess is supposed to meet me there. Caitlyn skips her art class to meet me in the library.

"How'd it go, dude?" She inquires. I let her know that I won't be seeing Ashley anymore. Caitlyn looks confused by this.

"It's because I'm in a wheelchair now so Doc doesn't think I need to see her anymore." My voice stumbles. Her brow furrows.

"Well, that's stupid." She says with emotion. She understands that I saw Ashley as a friend so it's a small loss. Caitlyn has homework pulled out to make it look like she is working on something. I look down at the paper resting on her lap. It's her Algebra 2 homework. She has a good portion of it done. The random numbers and letters look completely foreign to me. Caitlyn and I balance each other out. She is good in math and science and I do well in English and social studies. The bell rings and calls Caitlyn to her next class.

I stay in the library and wait for Tess to get here. She arrives just as the bell that signals class has started rings.

"Hey sorry. Running a bit late I guess." Tess says, handing me a cup of coffee from Dunkin Donuts. The warm paper cup heats up my cold hands. I set it between my thighs after taking a sip, so I don't spill it. She pulls out her phone and sets it before me on the table. "It looks like you have another appointment today. You're meeting Lynelle at 3:00." *Great.* I like seeing Lynelle but having two appointments in the same day is exhausting.

My backpack is hung on the handlebars of my wheelchair. I ask Tess to get out my English notebook. I still have the same assignments as the other kids in Mrs. Stark's class. I have a paper due today.

Tess flips to a tab in my teal covered notebook. The assignment is to write a farewell to her class as we end the semester. So, if you had a bad grade to leave it behind. If you did well to thank the material and move on to bigger and better things.

"As I say goodbye to Accelerated English 1, I look forward to what semester two has to offer me." I start the essay. "I thank this class for the opportunity of learning new things and for the empowerment I got from each essay." Tess scribbles all this down. This is the shortest and simplest essay I have written so far this year. I feel a bit of sadness as I realize I won't be having Mrs. Stark again next semester. I finish several minutes before the next bell rings.

In chemistry Charlie is already sitting at the back table. He has his test from yesterday in his hands. I get a glimpse at the red pen markings at the top. He didn't do too well. Disappointment is in his eyes.

"I'm sure you'll do better next time babe. Ask if you can retake it." I comfort. He smiles faintly at me. His eyes don't show confidence though. Mr. Vaughn is at the front of the class next to lab bench with a hot plate. He holds up a penny.

"I am going to turn this copper penny into gold." He dips the penny into a concoction of clear liquid. He then places it onto the hot pad. Steam sizzles off of it. Sure enough the penny is a shiny gold color. Very interesting. A group of kids line up next to the teacher with their own one cent pieces. Charlie goes up with our pennies. He brings back the changed effect from the science project.

A wailing sound alarms through the PSA speakers in the classroom. Fire drill. I feel panicked even though I know it's just a drill. Charlie instinctively grabs hold of the back of my wheelchair. He steers me out of the classroom once all the other kids evacuate. We stay close to the side of the lockers.

"You doing okay babe?" He asks. I give him a bent thumbs up. We are moving fast. It feels almost like a ride. When we are outside, we are directed to stay behind the parked cars in the employee parking lot.

The snow crunches under my wheels. Caitlyn and Ryan should be out here somewhere. Caitlyn has economics while Ryan has physics. I see a tall skinny kid wearing a Tigers sweatshirt move between people to get to us. Caitlyn is trailing behind Ryan.

"Why the hell are we having a fire drill in the middle of January?" Ryan's teeth are chattering as he asks. Caitlyn snuggles up against him for body heat. I press my arms to the back of my chair to try to preserve some heat myself. After about three minutes we are allowed back inside. That took up the rest of third hour.

I get rolled back to the library for math. I was handed the final to finish with Tess. I have to answer what the difference is between a tangent and a secant. This has to do with lines and circles. I tell Tess to write down one touches a circle a one single point while the other touches at two. The test was easy.

Fourth through sixth hour goes by slowly in the library. But before I know it, I'm in Lynelle's office ready for my appointment.

"Jenna, how's it going?" Lynelle pleasantly asks.

"I'm doing okay I guess." She is wearing a red turtleneck today. She crosses her legs in front of herself. I wish I could do the same. That position looks comfortable. I wonder what we'll be working on today. I take a glance at her notepad in her hand.

There isn't anything written down yet.
"Today I just want to talk. No psychology terms or skills. I just want to have a conversation." Her plan

throws me off. I don't know what to talk about. The silence in the room makes this very apparent. "Talk to me about your dad. I've met him once, but I still don't know him at all."

"My dad. Well, he and I are very close." I smile at the next thought that comes to my mind. "He taught me how to play cribbage when I was a young girl and now that's one of our favorite things to do."

Today Lynelle isn't writing anything down. She's playing a role of a friend rather than a therapist. I like this shift. I continue, "I came up the name for his bookstore. He opened it a few years ago after getting laid off at the papermill. 'Whitten's Written Word' he liked it right away. "

"I love that." Lynelle approves. I tell her about the time my dad and I went sailing on our lake and it flipped over while we were way on the other side of the lake and had to swim it back. I explain how I was in the back kicking while he was in the front dragging. We make a pretty great team. "How has your dad reacting to everything that is happening?" I had to think about that. He hasn't really said much about it.

"Okay. I mean he is like the strong one in the family while everyone else is allowed to struggle." Something I said makes Lynelle adjust her paper and pen.

"What do you mean everyone else is allowed to struggle?"

"Well, I mean mom is taking it really hard. Ryan is basically my twin, and obviously I'm the one directly dealing with it. So, dad feels like someone has to be strong so he seemed to volunteer." This is intriguing to her. She scratches all this down on her paper. She asks if this is fair. I think that's a rather strange question, but I answer it anyway.

"No. But he chooses that." I start to feel guilty about it. I mask this by frustration. "It's not my damn fault." I want to roll myself out of the room. I call for Tess. She comes into the room.

"Yeah?"

"I want to leave." I tell her. She looks concerned but she gets behind me and pushes me out anyway. In the car ride home, she asks what happened.

"Lynelle thinks it's my fault that dad is choosing to be strong through all of this. Well it's not." My messed up vocal chords are preventing me from expressing myself clearly with a proper tone. Tess just listens to me rant. "God, it's not like I like having this fucking disease." I end in a puff of breath.

"I don't think she meant it in the way of it being your fault." Tess says once we are parked in the driveway. I know she is right, but the anger doesn't leave me.

Tess steers me into the house over the ramp dad built. She places me before the stairs to go down to my room. She is behind me setting down my backpack before she helps me get downstairs. *Fuck this disease. I just want to be done with it. It's not my damn fault.* My thoughts swirl in my brain. I can't help but ruminate about it.

Tess didn't lock my wheels. I rock carefully back and forth. The chair inches forward. *Just do it, Jenna. Just do it.* I heave my body forward one more time and the chair and I go flying down six steps. I tumble out of my chair. A wheel knocks me in the head and runs over my body as it flings forward. My temple is throbbing. My vision tunnels.

"Jesus, Jenna!" I hear Tess call followed by quick footsteps towards me. I lay crumpled on the floor, the wheelchair several feet ahead of me flipped over. She helps me sit up. Tess helps me stand and shuffles me over to the couch. "What the hell was that?" Her tone is angry but that stems from the worry she is strongly feeling. I turn my head, avoiding eye contact with her. I feel tears slowly flood my eyes.

"I just want it to be over with." I sniffle. I feel the weight of the couch shift as she sits down next to me. She slings her arm around my shoulder.

"Jenna…" She takes a second to swallow her own tears. "I know you want it to be over but kiddo that is not the way." We sit on the couch in silence until mom comes home. "I'll be right back." Suddenly fear takes over my chest.

"You can't tell her!" I start to get emotional again. Tess confirms that she must. While she is upstairs, I wait, having a mini panic attack. I hear two sets of footsteps coming down the stairs. I meet mom's eyes.

"Jenna? Really?" Her tone is more on the disappointed side. I look away. I don't have anything to say about it. I worry for what may happen next. Mom gets Dr. Cooper on the phone. "Yes Doctor. I understand." She tells the phone set in her hand. I hear a muffled piece of advice. I catch the words "concern, help, and group". I have a clue as to what may happen. Mom confirms it. "Because of your incident Dr. Cooper is referring you to group therapy." I argue that I don't want to go but it's final.

25.

Tess takes me to the hospital at 7:00 the next morning. So much for sleeping in. The group is held in an enclosed patio. We are all circled up around a fire pit. There are seven of us here. Everyone seems to be close to my age.

 The therapist sits at what appears to be the start of the circle. Jamie is printed on his name tag. He has a pair of arm supports lying on the ground next to him. Tess placed me between two girls each older than me.

"Okay group. It looks like we have a new member today so you know the drill. Let's introduce ourselves." Jamie says. A girl with a bandana wrapped around her head starts.
"I'm Cindy. Fuck leukemia." Cindy is completely unphased by what she just said. A guy continues after her.

"I'm Andrew. Fuck! Fuck Tourette's." He looks to be in his early 20's. It's the girls to my right turn.

"I'm Payton. Fuck MS." I notice it's my turn. I suddenly am shy and feel uncomfortable.

"Um...I'm Jenna." I hesitate in case this is some sort of prank.

"And?" Andrew says.

"Fuck ALS?" Although my speech is still weak, I feel empowered. The rest of the group shares their name and what they have. It's not shocking that I am the only one with ALS.

The main disease is cancer. But even so we all have a chronic illness in common. Jamie ends the introduction with saying he also has MS. I soon learn that this group was more of a process group. We are allowed to share how we are feeling. A bitch circle some might say.

"The chemo is really bad." Cindy says. She goes into detail about how her barf has a chemical taste to it. "I'm hoping to get a wig soon. Just haven't gotten to it yet." I have an unfamiliar appreciate that my disease doesn't take away that sense of dignity.

"I can't use the bathroom alone anymore." I find myself saying without realization. Heads turn in my direction. They all seem to be able to do this simply task. "My caretaker" Tess perks her head up from her book. "Has to help me with just about everything."

The response from the group isn't so much pity as it is understanding cause they each have their own restrictions, whether that be oxygen tanks, some type of walking assistance, or even one kid needing a walking stick from being blind. Each of us are disabled in our own ways. Jamie responds to my vulnerable participation.

"And Jenna can you share how that makes you feel?" This isn't a condescending question. His goal is to make me be in touch with my emotions.

"I feel embarrassed, frustrated, helpless." I catch Tess's eye. She gives a slight nod showing she is sorry for my misfortune.

The group ends in an interesting way as well. We each get a small index card. We are instructed to put our diagnosis and our life span on it. Jamie pulls out a blow torch from behind his chair. He crumples his own piece of paper and throws it in the fire pit. We all do the same. He pulls the trigger that ignites the flame and just like that our destiny is up in smoke.

Tess drives us to school after the burning session is finished. When we are parked, she doesn't open up her door right away.

"Jenna, I want you to know that if I could switch places with you I would. You are so young to be going through all of this." Her words are kind, sincere. I don't have a good response besides to thank her. Caitlyn skips art class again to meet up with me.

"You really don't like art, do you?" I greet her in the library.

"Dude we have been drawing shoes for the past two weeks." She explains. Caitlyn is a good artist so I can see where her frustration of not being challenged comes into play. I redirect the conversation to tell her about group.

"Wait a second when did you start this? Why?" She asks good questions. I make eye contact with Tess. She gets the message.

"It was my suggestion. I thought it might help." Tess saves me from telling Caitlyn about the stairs event. I continue to tell her about the "fuck this" introductions.

"One guy was pretty cool. His name is Andrew. He has Tourette's."

"Is he cute?" Is Caitlyn's first question. I am thrown off by this question since we both have boyfriends.

"Kind of." I think about Andrew's straight, thick red hair, cut short on top of his head, and his astonishing eyes, one hazel and the other blue. His attractive features end with a dimple in his chin. "But why does it matter anyway?"

"Just wondering. There's no harm in window shopping." Caitlyn laughs after this remark. I guess she's right. I'm sure guys do the same thing. "Wanna go for a drive after school?" Sounds like fun. Tess says she'll join also. The bell rings to dismiss us.

It's the second week of January and this semester's English is on the main floor of the school. Ms. Jenkins is the teacher. Her class is on the smaller end. She removed some desks so I can comfortably fit my wheelchair.

It's been only a few days of having her as a teacher and I already don't care for her. She over explains things and hovers around the room constantly, causing for an obvious discomfort to all. She had us write a two-paragraph essay about ourselves, but the rubric was so strict the task was anxiety provoking.

We are assigned to do an "I Believe" essay. I decide to use this as an opportunity to communicate my strong frustrations with the class. By the end of the hour I have an acceptable introduction paragraph:

When it comes to writing, strict guidelines kill the potential of a good overall piece. It does not allow the person to be creative and have an open, free voice. The writer is too focused on the rubric. It is literally making the writer analyze every sentence they write, and it holds them back. There is a negative result from having a rather draconian form of instruction.

Along with this the atmosphere in which a person writes in is crucial to having a triumphant product in hand once finished. Finally, communication with all who are involved is deemed as the vital key to flourish in writing. I believe these three matters are lacking in second hour English class at Valley High.

I like this semester's lunch period a lot better. It's first shift and Charlie is in it along with the rest of the gang. Tess and I wait for Charlie where the two main hallways intercept, what the school calls the four corners. I am parked at the bottom of the stairs. Charlie grabs hold of the railing with his sweatshirt sleeve and slides down the stairwell.

"Nice stunt, huh babe?" I roll my eyes to his amusement. He takes over for Tess and rolls me down the hallway. Ryan and Caitlyn are already seated at a table.

We had to switch from choosing a circular table to one where my wheelchair can be parked at the end space. I wait there while my friends get their own lunch. Caitlyn knows me well enough to tell Tess what I would like to eat. I am brought back a spicy chicken sandwich with mayonnaise.

"So, we're going for a ride after school?" Ryan asks. I didn't realize he was invited. I catch Caitlyn's eye. She gives a shrug. I feel awkward since Charlie is the only one not invited. I opt out to not go. Charlie suggests for something just the two of us can do. He comes up with the idea of going to the movie theater.

"Sure. Sounds good to me." I agree. That means I get to add another movie ticket stub to my collection.

"I'm sorry Jenna, but I'm going to have to tag along." Tess says. I understand her reasoning for this. Plus, she won't be intrusive at all.

After school we decide to take Tess's car. Charlie and I wait for in the commons as she pulls her car around. One of us has to sit in the front passenger seat so we can fold up the wheelchair in the back. Charlie allows me to sit in front.

The movie theater is a matter of minutes away from the school. We are seeing a 3:30 showing of a kid's movie *The Odd Life of Timothy Green.* Charlie chose it because he knows my favorite actress, Jennifer Garner, is in it.

We get to the theater just in time to see the trailers of other movies run through. I feel bad that we must sit in the bottom section of the theater where you crank your neck up to see the screen. Charlie sits in the end chair so he could be next to me.

As each trailer plays, we give it a thumbs up or thumbs down depending on if we think it looks good or not. So far, a thumbs up has been given to the new *Harry Potter* film, *Bridesmaids*, and *Soul Surfer.* The only one that got a thumbs down from me was *Just Go with It* and that's just because it had my least favorite actor in it, Adam Sandler.

I decided to get popcorn and a cherry flavored ICEE. The movie starts with showing Jennifer Garner's character and her husband meeting with a social worker. The story unfolds to show how a child came into their life after trying years of conceiving, but this boy is different. He came from the soil from their garden and grows leaves on his legs. But just like with the seasons, as the leaves fall of the trees and changes into winter, his own leaves fall and eventually once they are all gone, he goes too.

The movie sparks something within me. Could this boy represent me? How I am also different, or rare? That my own differences will cause me to leave my family behind? I find myself crying from having this movie and character hit so close to home. Charlie rubs my leg in comfort.

26.

Group is every day in the morning. It means that I can go back to seeing Lynelle just once a week. When I get rolled in it seems that the seating arrangements have changed. Tess sets me next to Andrew. His neck is twitching.

"Fuck! Shit!!" He hiccups out. Today we are inside. The room is bare besides having us sit in our circle of chairs. I wonder how the session will start this time. Will we be damning our calamity again or will we hold hands in prayer?

The introduction doesn't fail my expectations. Jamie hands out a wheel that lists different emotions. There are five categories; sad, mad, joyful, powerful, and peaceful with similar emotions listed underneath. He has us scream the emotion we are feeling. He calls it the caterwaul check in. He starts.

"Cheerful!" He bellows out. The group claps in approval. Jack who has AIDS shouts shameful in a loud roar.

"Helpless! Fuck! Wanker!" Andrew exclaims. Andrew must have been wearing contacts before because today he has a pair of thick rimmed glasses. It gives him the sexy smart look. I am last to share. I take a deep breathe in preparation of getting a good yell out.

"Frustrated." My vocal chords allow for an expressive in-door voice. My peers hoot and holler in pride. Jamie rings us back in and explains what we will be doing today. He stands, bringing his left crutch with him, goes to the whiteboard in the front of the room. He writes an acronym on the board. DEARMAN is spelled out.

"DEARMAN is used to ask for something you want or need. It is a tool to help you be assertive. I think this is a good way to communicate with your treatment and support team."

He goes through each letter of the acronym. "D is for describe. With describing we are supposed to describe the situation we want to change but only use facts."

He moves down to write next to the 'E'. "The next letter stands for express. It allows you to express your feelings and opinions."

Assert is the third letter. He explains this is where you state exactly what you want. "R is for reinforce or reward the person if they were to do what you ask."

He moves down to the 'MAN' part of this acronym. "Being mindful is important because it keeps focus on your goal of what you want. Now, appearing confident is very imperative. You want to show you know what you want and why." He finishes with explaining how the 'N' stands for negotiating. "If you do this then I'll do that for you".

Jamie wants us to write our own DEARMAN for something we need from a person in our support system. After we write it out, we are to practice it out on a peer. Andrew and I pair up.

"Wanker! Do you want to go first?" He asks. His jeans have ripped holes in the knees. He's wearing soft padded gloves that come up to the second knuckle. Andrew lets his paper fall to his lap and he spastically smacks his forehead. I read what I have so far.

"Mom, you treat me like a completely different person now. You have said 'are your legs okay?' And not asked how I am doing." I move onto express. "That makes me feel like I am nothing more than my disease. I would like it if you ask how I am before you ask if my disease is acting up." I get to the R. "I would so appreciate it if you asked how *I* am doing." I pause before I move to the second half of the acronym. Andrew smiles a bit. He has been quiet so far. He puts up a wait a second finger.

"Shit! Beautiful! Wanker!" He verbally sneezes out. I hesitate in case he isn't done. His face scrunches up, as if he is about to say something else but after a few seconds the sensation goes away. He gives me a thumbs up.

"For the 'MAN' part I was thinking of saying what I want her to do one more time. And the last part is to negotiate. So maybe if she asks how I am doing I can return the question in a sincere way." Andrew puts his hand out for a fist bump. I hold up my crunched hand. He changes it to a high five. I pat my hand against his.

For Andrew's DEARMAN his goal is to have his younger brother to not trigger his Tourette's. I interrupt him.

"Wait, your brother purposely triggers your Tourette's?" My eyes shift between looking at each of his colored eyes. He nodes his head.

"Yep. He calls it Russian Tourette. Dickhead. Dick! Penis!" He explains that his brother cusses just to have him go off on spitting bullets of swear words. I shake my head in disbelief. That would be horrible.

Andrew breaks eye contact with me. His leg jogs up and down. "I hate--fuck! ---Tourette's. It is so--- wanker! ---embarrassing to be cussing all the time. Cunt!" Wherever he does cuss it sounds like an uncontrollable cough. Once he is done with sharing, we have a few minutes since others aren't finished.

"So how old are you?" I ask for an ice breaker.

"19. You?"

"I'm 17." He raises his eyebrows in disbelief. He comments on how young I am to have such a serious disease. "Yep. It's rare. I just got lucky I guess." I say sarcastically. He stares intensely at me.

"I want to hang out with--fuck! ---you. Sorry." Andrew does a side grin. I can't tell what his motive is. He pulls out his phone from his back pocket and hands it over to me. He wants me to put my phone number in it. I hesitate. *What will Charlie think of this?* I shove that thought away. Andrew is just a friend, someone to lean on and better yet give support to. Jamie groups us back up once he sees we are all done. I hand Andrew back his phone.

The session ends with us going around saying what we are thankful for. When it comes to my turn, I say my family.

When Tess rolls me out of the hospital my phone buzzes. I don't know the number. *See you tomorrow.* It reads. Someone briskly walks past me. It's Andrew. He turns around and winks at me. I smile to myself, but I also feel a small sense of guilt.

I don't get a whole lot school work done during my first few classes. Andrew and I have been texting back and forth all morning. It's fun to have a conversation with someone who gets it and can have fun.

> *Wanna know something cool about my disease?*

> *Sure. What?*

> *My Tourette's also comes out in German. Took it for four years in high school.*

> *Lol.*

> *What's something cool about yours?*

> *Ummm idk my caretaker is neatl.*

> *Tomorrow let's do something different during group.*

> *What's that.*

> *We trade diseases. I'll sit in your wheelchair, but you have to yell out curse words.*

> *Lmao maybe.*

The bell rings for lunch. Charlie meets me at the usual spot. He takes over in pushing my wheelchair again. Today I take note of that. Why can't he ever just walk beside me? I bite my tongue. He places me at my usual spot at the end of the table. When they go up I check on my phone that has been buzzing for the past few moments.

What's one thing you miss that your disease took away from you. Mine is having people be serious with me.

I take a second to think about that. Could it be clear speech? Showering? I got it.

Transporting myself place to place by myself. So, walking.

Charlie places his hand on the top of my head as he sets my lunch tray in front of me.

"Who are you texting there, babe?" He asks. I have a sudden unreasonable urge to lie.

"Nobody. Just someone from group." I decided to go down the path of honesty. He dismisses it. *Thank you, God.* Ryan and Caitlyn are discussing doing something again after school. My phone buzzes on the table.

*The group and I are hanging out
tonight. Wanna join?*

"So, Jenna you in?" Caitlyn asks. I totally spaced out
on what she suggested. All four of them are staring
at me, waiting for a response. This is the first time I
use my disease as an excuse.

"You know guys I'm feeling really tired. I think I just
want to head home. But you guys go ahead." Ryan,
Caitlyn, and Charlie nod their heads in
understanding. Tess holds my gaze. She's giving a
"we'll talk" kind of look.

Ryan and Caitlyn take the Audi to go who knows
where. Tess drives us back home.

"Okay kid. What's going on?" She calls me on my
crap. I want to act like it's nothing, but I know it won't
fly past her. We sit in a brief silence at a stop light.
She taps her fingers on the leather steering wheel. I
stare deeply into the front dash. I lean forward to
adjust the seat belt around my torso.

"The group from this morning is hanging out and I
want to join." I wait for her to respond. She laughs.

"That's great Jenna. Why didn't you just say so?" I
tell her that I didn't want it to seem like I was ditching
out on my friends. Tess seems to understand this.
"So, where we going?" I give her the address

Andrew texted me. It's 3352 Willow Street. That's off the main drag in Valley City.

The house is a dark green color with white shingles that stand out. The entrance has a three-step staircase along with a ramp. I wonder who's house it is. Tess rolls me up the cement ramp. I look down. There are chalk sketches of hop scotch and a family stick drawing. Kids must live here as well. Tess clicks the doorbell. Chimes echo inside.

Jamie opens up the door. I wasn't expecting him to be here much less it be his home. While balancing himself on his crutches he head gestures for us to come in. I hear voices in a nearby room. We are guided by the sound into the living room. It looks like I am the last one to arrive. Andrew glances over his shoulder.

"Fuck! Wanker!" He spits out. "Jenna, here." He scoots over his chair to make room for my wheelchair. He's holding several red cards. It looks like they are in the middle of a game. "Ever play Apples to Apples before?" I shake my head no. I've heard of it but just have never played it.

He explains it. We get several red cards that are a person or thing or event and then there are green cards that have a word. You throw in a red card that goes well with or describe that word that is on the green card. So, if the word is relaxing one might throw in massages. The person who reads the green card then picks which they think best fits.

"The person who wins--wanker! --gets the green card. Shit! You try to get the most green cards." Andrew slaps his forehead. Tess takes a seat next to me. Someone hands her a stack of cards. Mine read "New York City, immigration, Adele, barfing, the renaissance, Tiger Woods, and Kristen Wiig." The word we have to match is glamorous. I throw in New York City. It's Cindy's turn to pick which one wins.

"Here's what we have: Proposals, New York City, Channing Tatum, Puppies, Divorce, and Malls." Cindy weighs her options out. She turns over proposals and puppies. The next one out of the question is divorce. "Channing Tatum is the winner." Jamie raises his hand to show he put that one in there.

"Divorce was at least glamorous to me," says Payton. She's the oldest in the group besides Jamie. We all break out in laughter.

In the end a girl, same age as me, won. She has a feeding tube inserted. I forget what she has. It was a long jumble of consonants and vowels.

Jamie asks if I want anything to drink. I ask for some water. My throat feels dry. I try to swallow the accumulated saliva in my mouth. It's not enough. He brings back a water bottle with a bendy straw. Tess holds the bottle in front of me as I slurp away. I make the command to swallow but the water doesn't go down. It floats in my mouth. I don't know what to do. My throat convulses, spraying the water in front of me. It dribbles down my chin. A napkin is handed to Tess. I cough intensely.

"Just breathe. In and out." Tess guides. She wipes my face. I close my eyes. My brain strains as I try to swallow. Something seems to magically click, and I am able to swallow. Air gets pushed deep into my lungs with it. Tess is rubbing my back in a soothing motion. "You good?" I look up and see everyone staring at me with concern. I nod my head yes. "I think we should go." Tess makes up her mind.

"Jenna, I'll check in with you tonight," Andrew says before Tess takes me away.

Tess leaves after she tells mom about what happened. All the while I feel nervous because I know what that means next; another visit with Dr. Cooper. Mom makes an emergency call to him and we have an appointment set for the next morning.

 I skip out on dinner in fear of having something happen again. I go to bed early. I feel exhausted from the scare today as well as the fear of what may happen tomorrow. Tonight, I put the oxygen mask on just in case. My phone buzzes on my nightstand.

Hey you doing okay? It's Andrew.

I am okay. I have an appointment tomorrow and I'm kind of nervous. I'll be missing group.

Dammit. I was looking forward to you squawking out cuss words.

Sorry lol.

That's okay. You get some rest. If you need anything, I'm here for you.

I go to sleep with that secure thought that someone who gets it is there for me.

27

"This concerns me, Jenna." Dr. Cooper pauses. "But this was bound to happen. This is where this disease gets serious." I am prepared for his next blunt statement. "If you can't swallow, we are going to have to insert a feeding tube." I close my eyes, praying for all of this to just go away. *I want to die.*

Dr. Cooper prints out information on the procedure. My parents and Tess both came for this appointment. Mom sits next to me while Tess and dad stand. On the pamphlet it shows a person with a tube coming out of their stomach. "We are wanting to do this as soon as possible. It needs to happen." I want to protest. Mom puts her arm around me.

"So when will this be happening?" Dad asks. Dr. Cooper meets eye contact with each of us.

"Tomorrow." He confirms. I feel panic inflate my stomach. I don't know what to think. My logical mind knows I must do this and that it's inevitable. But on the other hand, my emotional mind is wanting to give up, to keep hold of the little dignity I have left. "I want you to go see Lynelle today. This is a big change." I don't want to go.

We schedule to come in the next morning at 8:00. I am to not eat or drink anything beforehand. Dad shakes hands with Dr. Cooper after the plan is set and stone.

We all came to the meeting in separate vehicles. Tess wheels me out the automatic doors of the hospital. Mom and dad give me a kiss before they head to work. We go to Tess's car that is parked in the handicapped parking. We pass by a guy leaning up against a brick wall. He steps out in front of us.

"Fuck! Pretty! How'd it go?" Andrew is wearing his sexy business glasses again. Group must have just gotten out as well.

"All well and good." I lie, croaking out a few sobs. I feel ridiculous crying in front of him.

"I thought you might say that. Emergency appointments-shit-- are never good." He has something behind his back. "I am hoping this might help." He holds out the children's book *If You Give a Mouse a Cookie.* I'm confused. He flips it open and starts reading. "If you give a mouse a--blow job--- not a blow job, a cookie, he will want---anal---milk." Andrew's body jerks and contracts whenever his Tourette's comes out. I find myself laughing. "If you give a---bomb--a mouse milk he might want--wanker gun--a blanket." Andrew hits himself with the hard-covered book. I am laughing hard at this point.

"Thank you. I get the point. I don't want you to hurt yourself." I tell him. He puts the book in the backpack he's wearing.

"I just wanted to make you smile." He shyly says. I appreciate him. A smile takes over my face. I don't remember the last time I laughed that hard. "When can we--fuck--not fuck hang out." I laugh once again.

"This weekend we can. I'll text you." Andrew walks in the direction of a red car. A guy who looks like he's quite older than Andrew is in their driver's seat. Tess rolls me away before I can get an idea as to who he is.

During chemistry Charlie asks me how group was.

"Good. Nothing special." I don't want him to know I was at the group event last night. He would ask about it and it would lead to Andrew. I want Andrew to be my special friend no one else's. He gets what it's like to have a disease that takes over his life. I want to respect how that bonds us, to keep that separate from the people who have no clue.

Mr. Vaughn is going through notes about precision and accuracy. My phone goes off. I glance at it.

"Jenna, phone. Put it in the jail cell." Mr. Vaughn says. *Dammit.* Tess brings my phone up to the blue cage set on Mr. Vaughn's desk. Charlie gives me a hard time about it by chuckling. He even pulls out his own phone and starts texting under the table. He turns his phone towards me to show he's texting me.

I'd bail you out if I could. I slap his leg. If I could flip him off I would.

I get my phone back once the class is done. I wait to check it in case it's Andrew. I feel guilty about it but I don't want Charlie to overreact. Charlie pushes me back to the entrance on my English class. He leans down to give a kiss. Usually he's the one to break it but this time I do. I want to read the text I got. Charlie gives me a weird look. I smile back and he brushes it off.

What's the difference between a snow woman and a snowman? It's from Andrew. *Snowballs.* I grin widely and laugh out loud at this joke. I put my phone away before I get yelled at again.

 Ms. Jenkins says today will be our last day to work in class for our "I Believe" essays. I just have the last paragraph to write for it. She lurks around the classroom, popping any one's personal bubble by poking her head over their shoulder. I finish my last paragraph with ease:

These three factors: a confining checklist for what needs to be in the paper, negative classroom surroundings, and ineffective communication leads me to my assertive stance that the Intermediate Writing class offered at Valley High is not holding to the expectations of what a higher-level English class should be like.

I turn in my essay and feel intrigued how she might take it. I said my peace though, that's all I'm happy about. I stare at the clock that is hung next to the door. A flare up of anxiety comes. Lunch is next and I don't know how I'm going to explain not eating.

When Tess and I go to the four corners to wait for Charlie I bring up my nervousness.

"What do I say to them?" I timidly ask.

"Why not just the truth?" *It's not that easy.* I shrug.

"I just don't want to worry them." Ryan doesn't even know I had an appointment this morning. I see Charlie coming down the stairs. I quickly shut the conversation down.

"Hey babe." He says, smiling. Tess is about to let go of my wheelchair to let Charlie steer, but I grab her hand. She gets the message and stays put. "Everything okay?" I nod yes. Tess starts to push me down the hall. Charlie once again drops my unexplained behavior.

At the lunch table I wait for how me not eating may play out. My anxiety rises. Before the disease I would be jogging my leg up and down but now I just have to sit with the discomfort. The gang comes back with plates full of food.

"Sis not eating?" *Oh, here we go.* I look to Tess for some help.

"She has an appointment with Lynelle after lunch. We were thinking of getting Subway afterward." *Thank you, Tess.* That explanation was all they needed.

I wait nervously in Lynelle's lobby. Our last encounter was rather negative. She comes out of her office and acts like it never happened.

"Jenna! Come on in. Good to see you." I hold my breathe. She gets behind me and steers me in. I feel my heart beating louder than normal. Lynelle moved the chair to the corner of the room, clearly out of the way. She's wearing white pants with a yellow top. She looks like she is ready for spring that is near. On her chair there are several pieces of paper. I can't quite figure out what they are from my spot. Lynelle notices that I am looking at them.

"This is what I want to work on for today." She holds up the sheets of paper. There are different colors of ink on it, some highlighted in bright yellow. "I want you to work on behavioral activities, or BA's and track them." I wait for her to explain. "A BA is something like reading, writing. But I want you to interact with other people as well, especially with your family. So, a card game or board game for instance." She turns the piece of paper around and sets it in my lap. Lynelle has a list of activities typed out. I must track them and get my parents to sign off once I do one. I see Lynelle fold her legs in my peripheral vision.

"Now with that aside." She gets my attention. "There are a couple things I want to talk about. The first is your procedure tomorrow." Dr. Cooper must have called her. "How do you feel about it?" For most of the day I have been distracted from it. That's thanks to Andrew and his funny texts. Lynelle suddenly brought me back to reality.

"I feel nervous." Is the first emotion I share. Lynelle nods her head in understanding. I appreciate her normalizing it.

"What specifically are you nervous about?" I take a second to place my finger on it.

"I think I'm scared of what that means, getting a feeding tube. Does that mean some other important task will go next? Like breathing?" I think of the oxygen tank at home. I feel my toes twitch in my shoes. I want to roll my ankle and crack it. I sit with the irritation.

"The other thing I wanted to discuss was what happened at our last appointment and what transpired after it." I knew she was going to go there. I stare at her blankly. "I didn't mean for it to sound like I was placing blame on you for how your father chooses to stand in your life. I apologize." I slightly smile to show forgiveness. "But my main concern is what you did at home afterwards. Are you suicidal?" She locks in with my eyes, seeing if she can get the answer before I can even speak. I look away. *Am I? Do I want to die? To kill myself?*

"Do I wish all of this was over with? Yes. But do I want to die? Not necessarily." I can see my response answers so much but not enough. Lynelle takes a deep sign, showing she was afraid but anticipating that response.

"Would you take your own life to make it end? I guess that's the real question."

"Right now, no." My honesty shocks me. She purses her lips together and nods. She turns the conversation to focus on how I am liking group. She asks if I have made any friends.

"There's this one guy. His name is Andrew." She raises her eyebrow.

"Andrew is a friend? Have you introduced him to your friend group?" I feel like I am getting caught in a lie. The same sense of guilt is there. I shake my head no. "Can I suggest that you do so?" The session ends with that hanging in the air.

28.

My phone goes off in the middle of dinner, a dinner I
cannot participate in. It's a small gathering strictly
family only besides Tess, as a sendoff as I go into
surgery the next day. What other appropriate way is
there to say goodbye to my ability to eat than to
have a feast? My phone rests lightly in my lap. The
touch screen illuminates. A message from Andrew.
My crippled hand swipes right.

You doing okay? Let's video chat tonight.

I tap on the respond box to be able to type. Mom
scolds me saying no phones at the dinner table.
Annoyed, I follow her direction. I don't know where
my mom's head was at when she made the dish.
Why have my favorite meal of homemade chicken
dumpling soup, when I can't eat it?

Ryan was told after school by my parents about the
feeding tube. He questions why I'm not telling
Caitlyn or Charlie.

"I will tell them. I just don't want to make a big deal
out of it. Ryan, please just keep it to yourself and let
me tell them." I say firmly. His eyebrows raise but he
nods in understanding. "Thank you." Mom and dad
downplay the night, keeping me from feeling
anxious about it. After they are done eating, we sit
around the table.

"Anyone want to play a game? A fun way to end the night and send us into the next day?" Dad suggests. Ryan smiles at me. I think I know what game he's thinking of. He runs down the stairs to our game shelf in the basement. When he comes back up, he has what I expected in his hands. We are about to play the game Catch Phrase. A flat sphere reads a phrase and the person holding it has to tell the other players what it is without saying the exact word. Ryan goes first.

"It's an addiction." He explains.

"Alcoholic." Tess guesses. Ryan shakes his head no. He looks straight at me.

"Mom is one of these when she goes to a city." I am completely stumped. Dad perks up with realization as to what it is.

"A shopaholic." Dad's right. It's my turn to go. *Tax Day* is read on the game's screen.

"The day we pay the government." Ryan guesses it right away. We don't play the game very long. My parents want me to get to bed. Tess insists to help me get ready for bed. She changes me into a comfy pair of pajamas. I then get wheeled into the bathroom.

Tess sits down on a bench stool in front of me. She squeezes toothpaste onto my toothbrush. I open my mouth for her to stick the brush in. She goes from side to side of my mouth, scrubbing each tooth till they feel clean. She holds a large plastic cup in front of me. I spit out the excess saliva.

I sit on the edge of my bed as Tess swing my legs onto the mattress. She then guides my back as I lean backwards into my pillow.

"Can I have my phone please?" I ask before she places the oxygen mask on my face. Tess raises a brow.

"I'll assume you want to text Charlie goodnight." We both know that's not what's going to happen. I bring my arms up to my chest. She props the phone up against my right hand. "Goodnight, Jenna. Say hi to Charlie for me." Tess winks before she leaves.

I click on the circular button at the bottom of the phone. I pull up Andrew's text from before. In the upper right corner, there is a picture of a camera. I tap it. A screen pulls up showing it is dialing Andrew. I wait a few seconds before he answers.

"Hey there!" He's shirtless laying on his bed. He has a tattoo on his chest. It's of a fiery sun inked in black. He runs his glove covered hand through his hair. "So, you doing okay?" He flinches and drops the phone. "Sorry about that." I can't help but smile. I feel my fingertips tingle as the phone lays against them. I try to stretch them forward. My phone tilts off my hand. I get hold of it again.

"There, now we're even." I shoot him a smile. "Yeah I'm doing okay, I guess. I'm feeling apathetic about it all. I just want to get it done and over with, you know?"

"Wow! Apathetic? Someone is-- wanker! --using their wheel of emotions." I roll my eyes at his comment. He grins a big toothy smile. His teeth are straight and white. He must have also had braces as a kid. "I want to--beautiful! --know more about you." I pause to think what to tell him.

"Well, I was born and raised in Valley City. Why is it called Valley City anyway? Our town's big "mall" is Walmart." Andrew rolls over on his side, hugging his pillow with one arm. I continue, "Umm I'm scared of the dark. Can't stand spiders. I don't know. What do you want to know?"

"What's your middle name?"

"Dawn. I hate it. I was named after dish soap." I scrunch up my nose in distaste for my middle name.

"Or Dawn like the first appearance of light before sunrise. Beautiful."

I return the question.

"James. Andrew James Peck." We get into a conversation about our first kiss. He had his at a campfire celebrating 8th grade graduation. "We burned a couch-shit! Have you ever burned a couch before? It--wanker! --makes the fire a bunch of different colors."

"I haven't but it sounds cool."

"What was your first kiss like?" I share my freshman year of kiss and tell. I dated the guy for a few months and then finally initiated it.

"I still remember the softness of his lips." I say, feeling tired. My eyes are heavy. We sit in silence for a little bit. I make a big yawn, my jaw extending all the way. Apparently, yawns are even contagious through phones.

"Jenna, get some sleep. You have a big day ahead of you." I'm too tired to respond. I hear him say goodnight before he hangs up the call. The phone tips onto my bed as I fall into a deep sleep.

29.

I am at the hospital at 8:00 sharp the next morning. Dr. Cooper is ready to do the procedure. I'm clothed in a gown. Dad sets me down on the hospital bed. A chill goes down my spine. My body doesn't react. I just feel a cold sensation go through my toes, up to my stomach and stops. An IV is inserted at the top of my left hand. I feel the pinch of the needle as it goes in.

"Ready to go, Jenna?" Dr. Cooper asks through a mask. His hands are already covered in surgical gloves. I nod yes. He brings a triangular mask up to my mouth. It covers both breathing apertures. My eyes gently shut. My body feels airy. *Lord, please guide Dr. Cooper's hands as he does this procedure.* I sink into a heavy unconscious state.

"Jenna?" Someone gently touches my arm. The hands are cold, rough. There is a tightness in my abdomen. I flutter my eyes open. Dad is standing to the left of my bed. Mom is behind him. My first reaction is to bring my hand up to my stomach.

"Everything went well." Mom grabs my hand and squeezes tightly. I notice Tess standing in the corner.

"I'll go get the nurse." Tess says and exits the room. I try to lift up my shirt to see the what it looks like.

Dad folds my shirt back. In the left upper quadrant of my torso is a circular piece of plastic folded over. It reminds me of what the opening of a blow-up beach ball looks like. I am intrigued as to how it works. A nurse followed by Dr. Cooper comes in the room.

"Jenna, it seems like you are doing well." Dr. Cooper praises. "Can you rate your discomfort on a scale of one to ten. One being nothing and ten being extreme discomfort." I rate it at a three. Doc tells us I can leave in a few hours. He wants to try the feeding tube out before we leave.

Lunch is set up at close to 11:00. They bring a bag of soupy looking food with a tube attached to the end of it. Dr. Cooper shows mom how to do it.

"You just connect this tube to her stomach, like this." I feel the plastic inserted in my stomach move a bit. Mom hold the bag of liquid above me. The food leaks into my stomach. The only thing I can feel is the slight jerking of the plastic cap. It's done in about ten minutes.

"All you have to do, Gail is juice up her food and put it in the bag." It sounds pretty simple. Tess looks intently at Dr. Cooper to make sure is getting it right. Dr. Cooper asks where my discomfort is now. I raise it to a four. He says that's normal, but I will get use to it. "Alright Whitten's you are all set to go. You have an appointment set up in two weeks from now and we will check how things are going."

We get down to the lobby of the hospital. My body sits heavily in my wheelchair. We are just about to exit through the automatic doors when someone calls out.

"Jenna. Wanker!" Andrew stands up from a chair in the waiting section. His tics seem to be very prominent today. His shoulders keep jerking up and down. "I just wanted to make sure you were okay." He has had to been waiting here for hours. Group gets out at 8:00 and it's quarter to 12 now.

"Yeah. I'm doing okay. Just a bit out of it." He nods in understanding. He walks over to where Tess and I are standing. He has something in his hand. It looks like a heart shaped box of chocolates. A sense of frustration comes over me. *What kind of sick joke is this?* He pulls off the top of the container. Inside in each cutout chocolate square is filled with a folded-up piece of paper. I take one out.

It reads *I'd rather be pissed off than pissed on.* It makes me laugh. I reach for another one. This one says *if you can't see anything beautiful about yourself get a better mirror, stare a little longer, look a little closer.* I get emotional.

"Andrew, thank you." I put out an arm to hug him. His facial hair that is growing out brushes up against my face. It's the same auburn color of his hair. He walks out with us and sits on a bench, calls for his ride.

Both of my parents go off to work and Tess takes over. In her car I sit there running my hand over my stomach. It feels weird having a protruding bump. I ask Tess to help me put a sweatshirt on before we go into the school. I don't want anyone to notice my new adaptation. I see Caitlyn in the hallway. She asks where I was.

"Can we talk privately?" We go into a corner of the library. I don't know the exact words, so I lift up my shirt slightly. Shock and concern are clearly expressed on her face.

"What the hell, Jenna?" I can understand her frustration. I can't find the right words to explain it. She sits there gazing at me. Tess sits and allows me to explain.

"Swallowing has become harder. We found out yesterday that I was getting this done and it just happened so fast." Now Caitlyn's emotions turn to anger.

"Why didn't you tell me?" Again, my words aren't there. I can't meet her eyes anymore. She folds her arms. Her nonverbals are very strong. She's wearing a black hoodie, one that makes her look a lot bigger than she is.

"I didn't want you to worry," is my best response. It doesn't cut it. She shakes her head in disbelief.

"Does Charlie know?" My lack of eye contact answers that question. I am afraid that he will try to take care of me even more. He told me he wanted me for me but lately all he caters to is my disease. He doesn't understand what this disease is doing to me emotionally. No one does besides maybe Lynelle and Andrew. One must by their job description and the other is living their own personal hell.

"Please let me tell him though." I plead. Caitlyn takes a deep breath in.

"Fine but do it soon." I let her know that I will. Caitlyn has a switch to herself. She can go from one emotion to the next without a huge transition.

"I'm just happy you're okay." Her tone is more relaxed. She glances at her wrist watch. The bell is about to ring. She swings her book bag over her shoulder. She caresses my hand before she leaves.

When we were younger, we went to this girl scout camp. There was a song that incorporated a goofy handshake. It took us awhile to get it down but once we did, we felt really accomplished. Ever since we used that handshake to show we have made up after a fight. I know that Caitlyn and I are okay.

At lunch I have to explain to Charlie that I'm not hungry. The table is quiet. Uncomfortable.

"Babe you should really eat something. You need to give your body energy." I feel like Charlie has become a third parent to me. I close my eyes in annoyance. Tess has been carrying around my box of "chocolates" around. I want to read one of the slips of papers.

"Charlie, you and I need to talk after school." Ryan and Caitlyn look down at their food. Charlie seems to be caught off guard, but he agrees to go for a ride after school. I ask Tess for it just to be us.

"I promise everything will be fine and each of us will have our phones just in case." Tess gets Charlie's phone number before she agrees to it.

In Charlie's car we pull over into a ditch on a backroad. I take a deep breath to prepare for what I'm about to say.

"Something happened a few days ago. And I was afraid to tell you about it." I start. Charlie adjusts himself in his chair to look at me. His seat belt is twisted around his shoulder. He gives a faint smile. I take a different approach to tell him about my feeding tube than show him it like I did for Caitlyn. "So you know how I've started group therapy?" He shakes his head yes. "Well, a few days ago I went to a hangout gathering with them."

"Wait was this when you said you were too tired to hang out?" He questions. I nod yes. I'm nervous to continue.

"Anyway, Tess and I went, and I was trying to drink something." Charlie comes to the conclusion himself.

"You couldn't swallow." He interrupts. I think it's a better time as any to show him my feeding tube. I use both hands to inch up my shirt just enough for it to show. He does a short gasp. I was expecting a reaction like that. He reaches over to touch it. As he grazes his fingers over it, I feel it push inward. I grimace at the discomfort.

"When did this happen?" is his first question. He moves his hand off it.

"This morning." He turns back to the steering wheel in obvious irritation. He glares through the front windshield.

"Jesus Jenna! What if something happened to you? I'm your boyfriend for crying out loud. I thought that meant something." He grips the wheel. I see his knuckles turn white. My phone that is in the cupholder buzzes. I reach for it. I bring it to my lap and see it's a text from Andrew. "Who the fuck can you possibly be texting?" I press the side button to turn it off.

"No one." I say quickly.

"No Jenna, you've been on your phone nonstop. Who the hell are you texting?" Before I can respond he takes the phone from my lap. He quickly reads the lock screen. He reads it out loud. "Hey there. Hope you are feeling okay. Let's video chat soon. From Andrew." He hits the steering wheel. It startles me. "Who is Andrew and why is he hoping you're okay? " He throws my phone down on the center console.

"He's a friend from group that's it." I try to defend myself as well as Andrew.

"You're telling me a guy from your fucking support group knew about your procedure before I did?" Charlie is getting more and more pissed off as this conversation continues. He runs his fingers through his hair. I reach over to touch him. He jerks away.

"God Jenna, I thought I was enough for you!" He says in an explosion of anger. I still don't have anything to say. He's fuming mad. "Well don't you have anything to say?"

"Charlie, I...I'm sorry for not telling you but I was afraid of how you would react. You're like another caretaker for me. What happened to being there for me and not my disease?" His eyes squint in confusion. "Lately you haven't been just my boyfriend. You have become too invested in my disease, not me."

"So, there is a problem with caring about you?" He isn't listening to what I'm saying. Frustration starts to flood me as well.

"No, I have Tess to take care of me. To push me in my wheelchair and feed me. I mean honestly if you had the chance, I am sure you would help me use the restroom." He glances back down at my phone as it goes off again.

"And this guy Andrew? Have you kissed him?" I feel offended that he thought I would cheat on him.

"Charlie are you fucking serious?"

"Well I mean you two seem to be pretty damn close. I have the right to question it." *A right?*

"I have the right to be friends with whoever I choose. I don't have to run it by you." My lack of voice is really frustrating me. I want to properly shout at him.

"Did he give you that box of chocolates?" Now I'm trapped. I'm honest and say yes. Charlie becomes quiet. He turns over the engine and starts driving.

"Where are we going?" I ask. He still doesn't say anything. I notice we are taking a route back to my house. He speeds through town and up the driveway. He parks the car and unlocks the door.

"Get out." He says coldly. I feel helpless.

"What? I can't."

"What now you want my damn help? Make up your mind, Jenna." He knows that's not how this works. He takes a second before he pushes himself out the door. He goes to the backseat and pulls my wheelchair out. He flings my door open. He's scaring me. Tears trickle down my cheeks. He slams his thumb down to unbuckle me. He picks me up in a hurry and sets me down. I get pushed inside the house. Tess is in the kitchen. She looks up from her food preparation.

"I need a break to figure this out. If you need help, try asking Andrew." He tosses my phone into my lap and with that he leaves.

Tess rushes over to me. My chest rises and falls as I gently weep.

"So, it didn't go very well?" She asks. I just want to go to bed, to wake up the next day and try again. This day has just sucked. Tess brings me into the living room. She takes a seat across from me on the couch. There's a box of Kleenex on a side table next to us. She takes a light sheet and wipes my tears. I can't even properly cry by myself.

"He found out about Andrew, didn't he?" Tess asks.

"Yeah but he's more frustrated that I don't want him to take care of me. I mean that's why I have you." I sniffle. Tess smiles at that statement. She likes to be there for me. I explain that I miss it when Charlie and I would just hang out when my stupid disease didn't get in the way. "The worse this disease gets the less of a romantic relationship we have." This realization startles me. I question if Charlie and I even have a relationship anymore. Once I am calm about the situation Tess goes back to cooking.

I finally have a chance to respond to Andrew. I see there's another text from him.

Will you be at group tomorrow?

I text him back yes. My chair is angled towards the front windows. I see the Audi pull up. Ryan and Caitlyn come in holding hands. I feel jealous of their easy-going relationship.

"Looks like dinner will be ready soon," Ryan states. Tess confirms that it will be ready any minute. Mom and Dad have to work again tonight. Caitlyn comes over by me. She can tell I have been crying.

"Hey you doing okay?" I shake my head yes. "You told Charlie, didn't you?"

"Yeah. He freaked out worse than you." She tells me she expected that. "So, did I but still." Caitlyn rolls me over to the dinner table. Ryan and Tess bring over a plate of grilled chicken breast and pasta.

Tess goes back into the kitchen to grab something. She comes back with my meal. Tess brings the tube that is dangling from the bag up to my stomach. She hooks it into my plastic port. The liquidy soup goes into my stomach. It feels weird getting a sensation of being full without having to chew anything. I wait for the others to finish their meal once my bag is empty.

The rest of the night is relaxing. Tess helps me get ready for bed again. We both know the routine very well by now. We are completely comfortable with each other. As I am laid down in my bed, I appreciate all she does for me. I want to somehow pay her back for it all. I have an idea as to how.

Andrew video chats me at around 9:00. He senses something is off right away.

"What's wrong? Is it your stomach?" He is wearing one of those shirts where it's cut on the sides. He looks to have just showered.

"No." I don't know why I don't want to tell him I have a boyfriend. I know I must tell him though.

"I didn't tell my boyfriend right away about the feeding tube and he saw that I was texting another guy." My voice is more quiet than usual. Andrew's tics are causing him to cuss a lot. He drops the phone.

"Sorry. Fuck! Wanker! Why didn't you--shit! -- tell him about the feeding tube?" I explain how Charlie has become another caretaker for me lately.

"He basically isn't a boyfriend anymore."

"And why didn't you --penis! --sorry, why didn't you tell him about me?" Andrew lays his phone down and turns on his side. His shirt droops and I see part of his chest. I don't know how to explain it because I know whatever I say won't justify it.

"I share everything with my friends and family. My friend group is my brother, my neighbor, and then Charlie. We are all friends with each other, but they have friends besides me. I wanted to have that. Plus, you understand what it's like to be living a personal hell." Even through the phone he seems to be completely focused on me. He's keeping eye contact and nods at the right moment.

"Jenna, what I'm about to say to you is very serious." His tics seem to cease. "Listen to me carefully." He takes a dramatic pause. "Life is your bitch." A rupture of laughter comes from me. That was just what I needed after this shitty day. Andrew has really come through for me today. I appreciate him. We say goodnight to each other. I put what happened today on the back burner and fall asleep.

30

Chemistry is uncomfortable now with Charlie. He
doesn't move to the back table with me anymore.
There is very little eye contact. When the bell rings
he rushes out the door. At lunch I don't go to the
cafeteria. Tess takes me into the nurse's station and
feeds me. I get a text from Caitlyn saying Charlie
didn't join them for lunch.

"Do you think I can fix things with Charlie?" I ask
Tess as she attaches the tube to my stomach. The
room we're in is small. There is a cot in the right-
hand corner for kids who are sick or have a
migraine. With my wheelchair there is barely enough
room to comfortably fit.

"I think you need to figure out what it is exactly you
want before you can answer that question." Tess is
smart and mature. What do I want? I think back to
group this morning.

***

*"Physically my leg is acting up with the MS. Other
than that, I'm fine. Emotionally I feel content yet
anxious."*

*"Content is under what core emotion?" Jamie asks.
The sheet with the four core emotions is handed*

over. She has to choose between anger, sadness, fear and joy.

"I guess I would say a mixture of fear and joy." It looks like she was the last one to go. Jamie turns the attention over to me.

"Jenna, good to see you. How are you today?" I share that my body is still getting used to the feeding tube. "And emotionally?" I turn my head and get a glimpse of Andrew. He nods his head as if it's a push for me to share the truth with how I'm feeling.

"I am feeling...remorseful, so under sadness, but also frustrated." It feels good to get it off my chest. Andrew lightly pats his leg in applause to me.

"Anything contributing to that?" Jamie asks. I share last night's run down of events.

"But then there's this other guy who seems to just get it. He's sweet and not condescending. Charlie is a good guy, but I think he sees me as a job that he has to take care of than a girlfriend."

Andrew is trying hard not to smile. He knows I'm talking about him and yet it's cute how humble he's being. Jamie opens this conversation to my peers. Cindy raises her hand.

"To me it sounds like this Charlie guy is scared to lose you." It didn't feel like that when he abruptly dropped me off. "I mean sure he got pissed off but I think that came from feeling betrayed. He can't get rid of the disease, so like they say if you can´t fight it, join it. He's taking care of you because that's the closest thing he can do to get rid of it." I never thought of it that way. I feel my heart soften towards the situation. "But, on the other hand, this other dude seems to be emotionally supportive. Very empathetic which I think is important considering all that is." My heart is at a tug-a-war again. The peer's response ends with that.

Jamie has us do an interesting assignment. We are to partner up and just rant to the other person for five minutes. But we must use ¨I feel-statements¨. Andrew and I naturally pair up. I let him start.

¨I--wanker--feel embarrassed that I am--shit--an issue for you right now." He slaps himself in the forehead. It leaves a red mark. ¨If I would have— Jesus." He screams while straining his body, ¨sorry, if I would have known you had a boyfriend I would have backed off." He unstraps his gloves and adjusts them tighter.

"I know. I'm sorry. I don't know where Charlie and I are at right now. I guess you can say we're on a break." Andrew is wearing a Tigers sweatshirt with

orange print. "You went to Valley high school?" He looks down at his shirt and gives a shrug.

"Yeah year of 09." I would have been a sophomore. He doesn't look familiar though. He goes on to explain he was kind of in the background at school. His Tourette's started during his senior year and caused him to be out of school a lot. "Can I be honest about something though?"

"Sure." I say. He adjusts himself in his chair and clears his voice.

"I noticed you. I was on the basketball team and I saw you during games. You were in the band playing the sax." This news catches me off guard. He knows me? "I thought you were cute." He wrings his hand around his neck. "And when I--wanker! -- saw you show up here I thought--shit! -- I might finally have a shot." His sincerity is sweet. He places his hands on the arm rests of the chair. He's taking deep breaths to calm down his nerves.

"Andrew, I need to think about all of this. I need to see how things go with Charlie before I can really respond to what you just said."

***

Once we are done in the nurse's station we go to English. Ms. Jenkins is at her desk, head down working on something. I'm rolled over to my corner of the room. My phone goes off in my lap. *I think we should talk after school, if you're up for it.* Charlie. I was expecting it to be Andrew. From the look on my face Tess is prompted to ask if everything is okay. I show her my phone.

"I guess I'll be meeting up with you at home."

31.

"So, what do you want to do?" Charlie asks after presenting the idea of breaking up for good. My heart is tugging at the strings of sorrow, guilt, and indecisiveness. Do I lose Charlie and feel sad and relieve him of his duties he has set up for himself? Or do I stay with him just for comfort? But that's not all there is to it.

The factor of Andrew is coming into play. There is something to explore there. Charlie stars at me in anguish as he sees me mull over my thoughts. "That's what I thought." He finally says.

"I'm sorry. But I would rather end it now where our friendship could possibly still survive rather than pushing those limits as well." He nods in understanding. His frown turns into a side smile.

"Well kid we had a good run at it." He kisses my hand. And there goes my heart string of relief. We are okay. I'm dropped off at home at close to 4:30. Caitlyn and Ryan come up from downstairs in hearing that I am home.

"How'd it go?" Caitlyn asks with her arm wrapped around Ryan's waist. I shake my head no. She comes to the side of my wheelchair and leans my head into her side. "You win some you lose some. Now all that's left to do is bone your hot ginger." I give a loud exhale of laughter. That does propose a question for me though. Is it wrong for me to start dating Andrew right away? I know we both want each other, but I feel obligated to Charlie to give it some time. I decide to give it a few weeks but that doesn't mean I can't talk to Andrew at least.

Since I finished dinner before everyone, I ask to be excused to go do homework. Tess brings me down to my room. She rolls me up to my white desk and sets my school books in front of me.

"Jenna, because I don't feel comfortable leaving you alone down here and that I need to help clean upstairs, I got a pager." She fastens this bracelet around my left wrist. "Press that center button and it will alert me or your parents. Okay?" I test it out right away. Tess's waistband beeps and she pulls out a small electronic box. She clicks it off.

I take out a book I have to read for English. I have to do a response on what I read. The book is *Night* by Elie Wiesel. I flip through the depressing pages filled with death and suffering.

The horror of the holocaust survivor makes me feel better about my own circumstances. It's a good twenty minutes before I finish the few chapters. I tap the button on my wrist. Within seconds Tess is in my doorway.

"What's up?" Out of habit I apologize for bothering her. "Jenna, please." I shake it off and give her the pencil I picked up with both hands. She repositions my wheelchair so it's facing her placement on the bed. Tess waits for me to begin.

"I believe that Hell is not just a place we may end up after we die. We each can be living our own personal hell without the act of dying. Elie Wiesel lived his in the holocaust. I am living mine through having ALS. But we each asked God's saving grace and got brought back up to Purgatory. I ask you to reflect on what your own personal hell is as you read my essay." Tess is still writing away as I take a second to feel confident with that opening paragraph. I look down to see the upside-down squiggles of her cursive writing, much more legible than mine had ever been.

"Want to continue?" Tess looks up. I glance to the left of her at the clock that is hung on the wall. It's only 8:00 but I feel beat. I come to the executive decision to call it quits. Tess changes me into a pair of cotton shorts and an old t-shirt.

"So, do you have anything coming up that's exciting?" I ask her as she wheels me into the bathroom to brush my teeth and comb my hair loose.

"My birthday is this month but that's about it." She seems unenthused by it. I smile to myself, knowing that I want to help make that day great for her. I look in the mirror that is the width of the wall it's placed on. This wheelchair feels like an electric chair waiting to go off rather than a walking assistance.

"What was your own personal Hell?" My reflection asks Tess's own. She's focused on picking out the small knots in the lower half of my hair.

"Probably the loss of my mother." She says glancing up and meeting my eyes in the mirror. I should have guessed. I feel completely insensitive. My mouth twitches at the pain from the tug of the brush. "Crazy part is she would have probably been the only one who could have comforted me through her death." Tess now displays her own apology of mentioning of the word death. "Sorry. Let's not talk about that. We are both strong living women." She ended the conversation by fluffing my hair one more time before bringing me to my bed.

The oxygen tank is set close to my bed. Tess places the mask over my face and lays the tube outside of my blankets. Goodnight wishes are shared before Tess is officially off the clock.

I fidget with getting my phone off the nightstand. I pull up the Amazon app and type in my search. A small picture of Julie Andrews and Jack Lemmon is displayed. I click the "buy now" button. My check out for the movie cost $163.69 but I found it to be totally worth it. Now I just need to figure out how to wrap it. Ryan should be able to help with that. After the purchase is made, I pull up Andrew's contact. I ring him to video chat.

"I broke up with Charlie." The glow of my phone barely lights up my face.

"Sorry to hear that. But as selfish as this is, I'm kinda happy." Andrew is in a comfy sweatshirt tonight.

"I understand. Can't wait to see you tomorrow in Group." I say before going to sleep.

32.

Today in group we are told family sessions are
coming up. Jamie further explains.

"Family sessions will be this week Wednesday. You
can have both parents here if that works with your
situation, but if only one can make it that's fine." Half
of the group looks comfortable with this, but the
other look bothered. Andrew is along with the later.
He's slouched down in his seat with legs spread at
shoulder width and his arms folded across his chest.

"Not looking forward to Wednesday?" I ask him
when we break up into pairs. Andrew stays
voluntarily quiet as best he can. He spits out some
cuss words. I wait for him to open up.

"My mother--cunt---left my dad and I because she
was too embarrassed to be anywhere with me." He
manages to say. His dad invited her to this family
session. "It's my fault she left--fuck shit---sorry"

"No Andrew, you're right that is fuck-shit. She didn't
leave because of you. She left for her own stupid
selfish reasons." I encourage. His face softens. He
likes the idea of me taking his tic seriously. His
hands twitch before him.

"I don't know. Anyway--fuck--- how do you feel about family sessions?" I want to cross my legs like a normal person and be comfortable, but my legs lay straight on the metal stands. I fold my scrunched hands in my lap.

"It'll be fine with my dad but not sure with my mom." I start. Andrew gives me his full attention, waiting for me to continue. "She can put on a front. Look happy when shit is hitting the fan kinda deal."

Jamie limps around the spread-out circle of us. I quickly switch over to the activity we're supposed to be working on and close my eyes. "My disability tells me I can't walk but I say that I am able of other things. I can still get from one place to another. My disability says I can't eat but I say I am strong with nutrition." I open my eyes to see Jamie smile in approval. Andrew winks at me for the good bullshit I just came up with. Jamie calls time is up.

Tess gets up from the back table. Andrew and I make plans to hang out after school before she takes me away. In the car ride to school, Tess states she will have to be there when I hang out with Andrew. I understand why and am not too bothered by it.

"What is your grade in art even?" I ask Caitlyn as she once again skipped.

"But it's not like I need to know how to draw a shadow to get by in life." She protests. I shake my head. *But you might need it to graduate.* She ignores my unapproving glance. "So, are you and Ginger are hanging out today?" I nod in excitement. Before I can tell her our plans the bell rings. I feel uneasy about going to Chemistry. I don't want to face the uncomfortableness that may happen with Charlie. When I enter Mr. Vaughn's room, I see Charlie sitting at my back table.

"Hey how's it going?" He asks with ease. Caught off guard I say I'm doing fine. "What?" He notices my pause. I shrug in not knowing what to say. "Jenna just because we're not dating doesn't mean I'm not going to be friendly to you. Besides who else will give you shit for whatever?"

"Caitlyn," is my response. He laughs at this.

"Well you can never get enough." Mr. Vaughn pulls up the practice questions on the SmartBoard. It's another balancing the equation problem.

"Yeah and in return I'll still help you understand this shit." I say nodding to the front of the classroom. Today our table isn't called to share aloud with the class. Charlie asks what my plans are for next week with my birthday. I totally forgot about it.

"I guess I haven't thought about it." *Will this be my last birthday? Will I only live to 18?* He realizes where my mind went.

"It'll be good Jenna, I'm sure of it."

The rest of the classes go by fast. Before I know it, I'm in the nurse's office getting my lunch. I go to the cafeteria once I'm done. Charlie chooses not to sit with us. Even though he and I are okay, I think he can appreciate what the vibe might be.

After school Tess drives me to Andrew's house. He lives past the ice-skating rink on the other side of town. I gaze at the tiger painted on the side of the ice arena. I close my eyes in remembrance of what it was like to skate. We turn down this long dirt road that's his driveway. Andrew is bundled up in a scarf, ticking away.

"You can't freeze the Tourette's out of you." I say as Tess wheels me up to him. Although his mouth is covered, I see his eyes smile.

Inside his house is very much log cabin. Over the fireplace is a deer head. It's an eight pointer. His living room is sunk in with a carpeted step around the circumference of it. He sits down on the long beige couch. With arms around my torso, Tess helps me step down and gets me over to where he is sitting.

Andrew rests his arm along the top of the couch.

"I want to show you my favorite band." He states while flipping his laptop open. The screen is cracked. He must have dropped it. "Damn Tourette's." He points out. With the computer turned towards him, he types something into the search bar. A piano plunking out quarts notes plays with a synthesizer in the background. "Blue October, ever heard of them?" I shake my head no. I listen to the lyrics.

The song is about feeling broken and trying to pick up the pieces. I relate to it. Andrew smiles as I bob my head to it. He turns the laptop towards me once the song is finished. "Play me something you like." I pause to think of what to show him.

"Okay but you can't make fun of me." He grins to show no promises. The computer whistles.

"You know I can't smile without you. I can't smile without you. I can't laugh and I can't sing. I'm finding it hard to do anything." The first verse plays.

"Barry Manilow. Ever heard of him?" Andrew says he hasn't.

"But I like it. Very late 1970's"

"I'm embarrassed. People think I'm too old school for liking him but he's one of my favorites. Thanks for not laughing at me." Andrew comes closer to me. With a hand on the side of my face he leans in.

"Well, I truly can't smile without you so…" and he kisses me. The hairs on his upper lip brush against my cupids bow. A sense of guilt comes over me.

"Andrew." I gently push him away. "Maybe we can take it slow, okay? Since you know?" With some disappointment he agrees.

"Sorry. Couldn't let that moment pass I guess." His eyes are focused on the floor. *Screw it.* I lift up his head and kiss him patiently.

"You're right." I say while unlocking my lips from him. Andrew finishes the moment by playing "What a Feeling" from Flashdance.

33.

Tess has the morning off since my parents are coming for group. The chairs are spread out in a semicircle with Jamie in the front to give directions.

"Parents or guardians, I am so happy that you could be with us today." Instead of Jamie's usual sweatpants he stepped it up to jeans. "Through this therapy we have been working on processing our illnesses and what it means to us. Today they will share with you what that is."

We break off with our family members around the open space of the room. Dad grabs the two chairs for himself and mom and plants us near the windows in the front of the room. We sit in a triangle.

"Well, want to share with us what you've been working on?" Mom asks. She's baring a bright smile for no one to really notice. *Great, here we go.* I reposition my chair so it's a foot more away from them. I suddenly feel annoyed.

"This disease sucks, what do you want me to say?" Mom swallows and readjusts her smile to one without her white teeth.

"Honey, I know. But this time is for you to talk to us about it." My stunted emotion softens.

"You know our doormat that says happiness? Well that word just seems to be a doormat to me now." Dad's head falls to the floor. His hands twist in from of him. He looks like he's trying to keep it together.

I try to find Andrew and his parents. They are on the across from us near the entrance of the room. I catch his eye. He looks to be having just as much of a miserable time. A tic breaks our eye contact.

"I'm not supposed to die before you guys. That's not how life is supposed to go." This breaks mom now. *Shit*. She takes dad's hand in her left and mine in her right. We must look like a prayer circle. Mom doesn't say anything. She just squeezes our hands and looks down. Maybe she is praying. "I'm sorry guys. It's just that I am sick and tired okay? I am so tired of all of this." They both look up at me and nod in understanding.

"We know honey. We know." Mom says, trying to let that smile reappear. I take out a piece of paper that's in the pocket of my hooded sweatshirt. I start to read.

"Things have been tough lately. I can't walk or eat properly. My disease has taken away both of those abilities. ALS can take away my hands, my speech, and even my breath but it cannot take away my strength. I may die but it cannot take away my life. My life is something that will always be there. I have lived, made connections with people, made memories. It will never be able to take that away from me. I thank my parents, my friends, my support team for what they have given me and what they have contributed to my life. Although I may leave soon, my life will never be over." My mom first, but shortly after my dad loses it too. Jamie calls time.

"I hope this session was beneficial to all of you. Group I will see you tomorrow." He excuses us.

Andrew and I text later that night. I invite him to the birthday get together we'll be having in two days. He says he's excited to come. I am less enthused.

34.

Everyone is seated around the dinner table which is covered in a gray tarp. Since a meal would be inappropriate, mom has a craft for us to do to celebrate my birthday. We each have a small canvas in front of us. Running the length of the table in the center are bottles of acrylic paint. We each have a red solo cup next to our canvas.

"Tonight, we are going to do acrylic pours." Mom pridefully states. I have never heard of this. She brings up her own cup. She picks from the assorted colors in front of her. After adding all of her chosen colors she takes a white cylinder that holds Modge Podge.

A bunch of unsharpened number two pencils sit in their own plastic cup. She stirs her mixture and flips the cup onto her white square. She lifts the cup slowly. The colors expand into a unique pattern. She then lifts up her canvas and tips it. The paint goes in the direction of gravity. This does actually look fun.

 Ryan takes my cup and asks what colors I want. I point to a bright pink, soft blue, vibrant orange, and a neon green. He adds in the Modge Podge for the magic to happen. He places the cup in front of me so I can stir it all together.

"Ready?" Ryan asks before setting the cup on my canvas. Once lifted the paint spreads out to make a wild design. I look over at Caitlyn's and she is in the middle of finger painting penisis into hers. I like her idea and decide to do something similar. Mom, predictable enough, wrote "faith" into hers. I'm thinking of a different "F word".

After we are all finished Dad tears paper bags in half and lays them on the island for the paintings to dry.

Mom, being the organizer, says it's time for presents. Clever enough everyone gets out their gift that's placed in a bag. No wrapping paper involved. Tess hands me her gift first. Pulling the tissue paper out I reveal a new cribbage board that is in the shape of a '29'. Andrew is next.

"Since you seemed to like them so much." He states after seeing it's a Blue October CD. The other gifts include a necklace, a new shirt, and a note from Caitlyn saying she'll smoke me up before I die. Mom and dad's gift is last. They tell me to close my eyes. I hear them walk into a different room. They say ready a few seconds later.

I open my eyes to see dad sitting in a motorized wheelchair.

"We know how much independence means to you. So, we thought we could help out with that. Tess helps me get situated in my new ride. I steer myself to the living room and around the two couches. This gift really is great. After warming up to it for a few minutes the party ends.

Once everything is cleaned up, I ask Ryan to help me with something. Downstairs in my bedroom I explain the task.

"Tess's birthday is coming up and I wanted to get her something nice." I show Ryan the movie. He's never heard of it either. I point to an old science book that's on my bookshelf. He grabs it and notices how light it is. Flipping open the front cover he reveals the reason why. The book is hollow.

"When did you do this?" is his first question.

"Years ago. It's where I hid my diary when I was a kid." That explanation has Ryan back off. I ask Ryan to wrap the movie in regular wrapping paper. We then place the package in the book. Now for the fun part. I take the sleeping bag off a small pillow I have. The book goes in the bag. "In my desk drawer there should be some duct tape." Ryan gives me "you've got to be kidding me" look. I swat my fingers at him.

The raucous rip of the duct tape sounds. He blankets the book in it. I ask for him to put it on my bed so I can write my "From and To" on it before going to sleep.

"Alright, goodnight weirdo." Ryan leaves me after helping me get comfortably situated in bed. "From Jenna" in black sharpie is doodled across the front of the obnoxious package. *Now how's the for character, teachers?*

35.

I franticly stab my finger against my call button on my wrist. My lungs feel like they're on fire. My chest feels tight. I look down at my oxygen tank and the black dial is in the red zone. The orange light above it doesn't glow. I press the mask to my face and try to breathe. I manage to take the bracelet off and pound with two fingers it's middle button. *What the fuck is wrong with this thing?* My vision starts to tunnel. *This is it.* The last grains of sand are falling to the bottom of my hourglass. My time is up.

Made in the USA
San Bernardino, CA
06 February 2020